Snowflakes

Snowflakes

an anthology

Edited by Debz Hobbs-Wyatt and Gill James

Bridge House

British Library Cataloguing in Publication Data

A Record of this Publication is available from the British
Library

ISBN 978-1-907335-40-2

This edition published 2015 by Bridge House Publishing
Manchester, England

All Bridge House books are published on paper derived
from sustainable resources.

Contents

Introduction

At Bridge House we love putting together collections of short stories. We like to launch them around Christmas time. We love the idea of the Advent Calendar. A story for every day from the 1st to 24th of December.

This year we asked for snowflakes – those unique droplets of frozen water that have glorious patterns and give life as they melt. That wasn't an easy task for our writers yet they met the challenge.

These stories aren't sentimental. They make you think and they may take you a little way out of your comfort zone. Some have upbeat endings, some leave us wondering and some make us a little sad.

As usual we've enjoyed working with our authors who have engaged enthusiastically with the editing process. We've been impressed with their professionalism and their enthusiasm.

Early next year there will be a call for submission for our 2016 anthology. Do look out for that.

We hope you enjoy reading this collection as much as we enjoyed putting it together.

Happy reading!

Siren

Christopher Bowles

And hers was a haunting song.
It was a lilting melody that span threads and knitted
  parchment.
It was an aural tapestry of worn history.
Of fragmented memories snatched from birth...
...All the way to the final pleading cries to an absent
  god on a deathbed.
And it was a song that everyone heard differently.
It was a song meant for one.
An individual.
Each verse as perfectly crafted for every imperfect
  person.
One song for every sad little life.
And the simple way in which it was snuffed out.
And hers was a haunting song.

Samson was officially missing on Wednesday.

The last time I saw him was on Sunday night, when he slept beside me. I liked to watch the gradual rise and fall of his chest. The way his feet never warmed up. The tickle of his stubble. I liked to lie with my face close to his. He'd breathe on my cheek, and I'd know he was alive. Alive and there. There beside me, here with me.

When I awoke for work on Monday, he'd already gone. Nothing unusual, sometimes he had obscenely early meetings. Heaven knows we all need our space from time to time. But as I commuted, shuttling along in a steel carriage, watching the rest of the Londoners mill around like ants, there was a tiny pang in my side.

I was stood, holding onto the strap, bobbing along

with every jerk of the train, and I caught the eye of a sad looking woman. Late forties, maybe. Shawl. Leatherette clutch bag. Clumpy shoes. With every breath she released, another cloud of frosted air. Her eyes flickered away quickly, and I couldn't help but feel sorry for her.

The train emerged, an unblinking metal shrew above ground, and I was surprised at how clear everything looked. As the trees and rooftops cantered by, I watched the first snow of the season begin to descend through the misted glass. I began to wonder how thick it might fall.

Would it settle?

After I got back, I cooked, and fumed aloud about the day's woes to the cat, who lovingly curled around my legs in sympathy. And I waited. But Samson never came home. I drifted off to sleep fully clothed on the sofa, and when I awoke, I was still there. He hadn't arrived safely under the cover of darkness and carried me to bed. The sheets weren't crumpled. Hadn't been slept in.

I called. And I texted. But nothing. No response. Just the stark void stretching out after the voicemail. I tried not to sound panicked, and left three messages throughout the day – once before work, once on my late lunch-break, and a third after I arrived to a still empty house.

Nothing.

So I filed a missing person's report. And on the Wednesday morning, I stayed home from work to answer questions to a policeman who looked particularly unconcerned with my plight.

When was the last time you saw your husband?
Had you been fighting recently?
Any recent troubles in your relationship?

Were either you or your husband under any unusual levels of stress?

Any issues at work?

What was he wearing when you last saw him?

Every question was asked with the subtlest glance at a watch. Or a faint roll of the eyes. Or a yawn. Just a series of tiny yet vaguely perceptible acknowledgements that neither I, Samson, nor the case was worth his time or attention.

And so I answered his inquiries. And I watched the young policeman go.

And then I sat down, stroking the cat until the tears came.

By the time Friday had come around, I was a mess. I was a shattered version of my former self. Pieces of my body, glued back together, barely functioning. I had trouble eating properly. Difficulty sleeping. Constantly worrying, looking at the clock. Watching the mail pile up at the front door.

Second after second. Minute by minute.

I always kept it unlocked, for him to simply wander back in. Whenever I forced myself to cook, I always made an extra plate, and kept it for him. It mostly ended up in the bin. Sometimes in the cat's bowl if he was lucky.

Hours and hours and hours. Days.

It wasn't until Sunday night, when, after no further attempt from the police to contact me, that I began to feel truly alone in this crusade. What had happened to my husband? Why was no-one interested in finding him?

And so I started my own investigations.

I searched his bedside drawer, tipping it out onto the made bed. Nothing out of the ordinary. Socks. A well-thumbed novel. A handful of coins. A comb. An embroidered handkerchief.

Where are you?

What aren't you telling me? What aren't I seeing?

A cursory glance at his wardrobe. Nothing special missing. Just the clothes he disappeared in. A standard dark brown work suit. His everyday dress shoes were missing as well. The red tie. I rummaged through the rails, and came up empty handed.

In the hallway, I opened all the mail. Water bills. Electricity bills. Telephone bills. Internet bills. But nothing of use. No bank statements which could be used to show he was still withdrawing money, alive, hidden somewhere. No postcards in his familiar spidery scrawl.

I searched the pockets of his coats, and found, once again, nothing. I threw them to the ground in frustration, and something slid out from an inner nook – some secret cranny I hadn't known existed, stowing away under the hallway table. It was only small. A scrap of paper, maybe?

I reached out with shaking fingers, and pulled the mystery item into the light.

A matchbook.

Opening the card sleeve, I saw it was empty. All the fires had clearly been lit. I turned it over in my hands. Two gilt words printed in silver on the cover. The name of a bar, or a hotel perhaps?

Come Hither, it said.

The club was everything I expected it to be. Rampant with sin. Rotting from the inside out in a garish masquerade of colour, nipple tassels and empty bottles. There was a haze over everything.

The music pounded. A heartbeat pumping through my body. A rhythm. Blood.

I peered through the crowds, but could not see him.

Off to my right, a cheer surged through the room, and one of the podiums was suddenly lit up like a beacon, revealing the pole, and the young, doe-eyed girl perched upside-down at its apex. Hanging with an air of nonchalance by her legs.

Another dancer appeared to my left. This one astride a mechanical bull, full-lipped and bursting out of a denim jacket. I peeled back my lips in distaste. A grimace.

A third, dressed in the traditional garb of the season. A Santa hat and a scarlet thong. What else?

Was this what Samson liked? Had he come here, desperate to get a fix of these free and wild women?... Was I not enough?

The thought was sobering. None of the bar staff could remember anyone fitting Samson's description, and the dancers were under some kind of shroud of secrecy. A Hippocratic oath for the sexual healers.

I was about to leave, when something pulled at my periphery – a glimmering, begging to be noticed. *Yearning.*

The door in the dankest corner of the filthiest pit.

It was inconspicuous, tucked away in a corner, past prying eyes and shielded by the nimble bodies of the whores.

Cabaret Lounge, it said.

Come Hither, it said.

The handle was surprisingly cool under my touch. It opened easily.

Up a flight of sound-proofed stairs, climbing into the unknown, I could feel it. Samson. He was here. I just knew it.

I emerged into a dimly lit atrium. A grand, weathered

stage stood proudly at one end of the room, the wall behind it swathed in thick, crimson velvet. The stage-front rippled over into a short staircase, and emanating from it were tiers of private booths. Each intimate cocoon boasted a table, just large enough for a single chair, and a lone figure.

Men.

Fraught and broken, wearing crumpled suits and tear-stained masks. Each of them staring down at their drinks as the ice melted. Or their phones as they rung out in their hands. Or twisting their wedding bands on their fingers. Or opening their wallets and looking at the pretty pictures of people they sort of knew. Half remembered.

They were like an ocean of puppets. I waded amongst them, searching for a familiar face, a safe harbour. A lighthouse. But I found only the blank faces of strangers lost at sea. All bobbing along to the same invisible tune. All clutching their belongings and half-filled glasses like the shipwrecked cling to driftwood. All weeping silently. The taste of regret hung heavy in the air, and my tongue was coated with it, thick and smoky. Charred wood.

And so I came across the only empty table, and sat, gingerly, staring around at them, desperate for a glimpse of Samson. It wasn't until I actively began my search, that I realised just how many tables there were. Close to a hundred, maybe? One hundred poor souls, all drowning their sorrows in a forgotten room.

On the table, there were three things. An unlit candle in its holder. An ice-bucket with an open bottle of champagne and an unused flute nestled firmly inside. And a matchbook branded with the bar name. Black. Gilt silver printing.

After a few moments of hesitantly looking around, my eyes rested upon the champagne. I knew it wasn't mine to take. But the previous owner was nowhere to be seen. No coat or bag or gloves left at the table. No mobile phone. And so I removed the flute, and poured myself a glass.

It fizzed delicately. Still bubbly – only recently opened; as if in servile expectation. It had a tinge of pink to it. Like the first moments of a blush on a young girl's cheek. I smiled to myself, and sipped it tentatively.

And then, movement.

A spotlight appeared on the stage. The house lights went down, and only the tiny pinpricks of candle flames floated around me in the darkness.

The curtains parted, and she appeared. The woman. She, with her long dark hair, down to her waist. A red dress, slit to her hips at both sides, and plunging down to her navel in front. It glittered under the spotlight. And a hundred little fires were reflected in her body as she moved to the front.

The silence was palpable. I was aware of ninety-nine other voyeurs leaning in expectantly. And curious, yet vaguely horrified, I too was drawn to her.

She sang.

Her lips parted, and she sang.

It was a song of love. Love earned, blossoming, withering on the vine and dying. She sung of divorce. She sung of sadness. Of nights spent alone in front of the television, microwaved meals on laps and the smell of stale sweat. She sang of dark thoughts of revenge. She sang of twisted fantasies, of imagined rapes and punishments.

And as she sang her terrible song, she moved amongst the tables with ease, and a hundred pairs of eyes watched her intently. She trailed her hands over the backs of chairs and moved towards a man in the back, who was cradling a whiskey and crying.

And as she sang the song, he was moved by her. Something resonated in him, clicked into place. She held out one hand, and he took it, and rose from the table. She smiled emptily, and reached out, snuffing the flame of the candle on his table. Leading him back through the ocean of unhappy men, she lilted, and trilled and was every picture of the doting songbird. A caged bird with a fixated, hungry gaze.

And when she reached the stage, she passed through the curtains, and he followed. The heavy red velvet barrier fell back into place. They disappeared into the void.

I sipped my champagne uncomfortably, alone with my thoughts. No-one had applauded. In fact, as soon as she had selected him, nobody else seemed even remotely interested. They were simply all too wrapped up in their own little worlds. Their own tables. Personal domains. A private trap with no bars.

I toyed with the matchbook. Rolling it around on the tablecloth. After a few moments, I plucked a match from the card fold. And I grazed it against the rough patch on the edge. It sparked to life, I touched it to the wick, and the candle was lit.

I returned to sipping my champagne.

I don't know how long passed. But I wasn't under any urgent need to rise. I didn't want to leave. I just wanted to rest.

No.

I wanted to wallow. In this room, so heavy with grief, I wanted to cry. I wanted to vent. I wanted to rage and scream, and shout and weep and beg him to come home.

But instead, I sat there, shaking quietly to myself. Sipping blushing liquor from the glass.

After a while, there was a noise. A muffled bang. I looked up, only vaguely interested. And then, in the doorway, a young man appeared. He was blonde, had a fairly plain face, but seemed in obvious distress. He took a moment to survey the scene, and puzzled, eventually stumbled towards the only empty chair in the room; right at the back.

After a few moments, she emerged again. In her daring red dress. And the candlelight radiated from her yet again, and she moved to the front of the stage and began to sing.

She sang of determination. Of ambition. She sang of justice. And righteousness. And then she sang of dark dealings. Of under-the-table handshakes, of warfare and treaties. She sang of broken swords. Of tipped scales. Of rigged dice.

And as she sang her lament, she moved to a table not far from my own. And she extended her hand and he took it, and rose from the table. I recognised him. It took a few moments, but eventually I began to see him for who he was. Who he used to be.

That sarcastic young policeman. The one who had questioned me a few days ago. The one who obviously never cared. I watched him as he watched her. As she snuffed out the flame. And I watched him follow her through the maze of furniture, and cross the thresh-hold between the heavy curtains. And I watched them swallow him.

I reflected on my life. On the dreams I once held so dearly, but left to die on the wayside. I remembered the first time I saw Samson. I remembered our wedding day. I remembered the sacrifice.

And then I watched as the blonde man who had arrived after me played with a matchbook found on the table, next to a bottle of beer he was happily drinking. And I watched him light the candle.

And, like clockwork, that muffled bang as the door downstairs slammed shut. A new face emerged into the theatre, and sat down at the now vacant policeman's table.

Come Hither, it said.

I heard her before I saw her.

And she sang a terrible song. She sang of an unhappy marriage of convenience. Of a wedge driven into a holy union, and a void left behind. She sang of loveless, carnal affairs. She sang of the cheating husband. The dutiful spouse who faked ignorance.

And then she reached his table, and Samson rose to take her hand. And she doused his candle, and led him through the crowd, and I cried into the ice bucket as he left me.

I watched them leave, one by one. And I heard all of their stories.

I have heard the songs. The lullabies, and the love sonnets. The happy romances and the uplifting ballads. But I have also seen the sad faces at the end. The crushing defeats. The depths of the heart.

I counted each one as their candles were put out. As every light was extinguished, and they disappeared with her, behind the red curtain. I watched their places all in turn be filled again. A new man to step into the shoes of the old. The candles relit. The cycle continues. The big wheel turns.

And so I sit. And I delicately sip my champagne.
And I reflect. And I cry.
It will be my turn soon.
And I await it eagerly.

About the author
Christopher graduated from The University of Manchester with a B.A.(Hons) in Drama, and has since taken a rather theatrical approach in love, life and languor. Even as a child, he would collect lost keys, and attempt to open doors in strange places, hoping to come across hidden worlds and Wonderlands. Nowadays though, he's happy to simply curl up with a warm blanket, a good book, and cake. Lots of cake.

Undertow

Clare Weze

"Dead, huh?" As opening lines went, Huey's surely couldn't be beaten, and as she turned around his hunch was proved right; she was Japanese: the slight frame, the jet waterfall hair, the exquisite neatness of the foot next to the two fish.

"Yup. Poor things." The wind took the end of her words – with their British accent – as if what was about to happen to him came in a squall from the sea, was already known deep under that water.

Huey always came to the shore at this bearable hour with families gone and the barbecue hardcore not yet begun. He'd found her watching the waves break out of the black water in just the place where he liked to stand and do the same thing. He wanted to laugh.

Instead, he focused on the fish: jellied around the gills but no sign of bloat yet. "A pair. Makes you think they must be family."

She smiled at him. Her long hair coiled around itself in the wind, and with her skirt clinging to her legs, the mermaid silhouette was right there. If not for the fish, those might even have been his first words to her: *You look like a mermaid.* His mermaid. And then the small talk he'd prepared surged out automatically, no problem, smooth as chocolate and no mention of mermaids.

She listened and laughed in all the right places. Then she said, in her beautiful voice, "You really live here?"

Huey nodded slowly, squinting at the headland.

"Oh, it's so beautiful." Her smile was wide open, couldn't fail to reassure, but it toppled his nerve. He filled his lungs, seeking calm, and for the first time caught the

19

smell of the fish. Tar, too, from somewhere close by.

He took her for a coffee at Carido's on the boardwalk. They chatted easily. There were always music interests, but he didn't need to fall back on those; they just got along. Josh, her traveling companion, had gone on to Vegas, but Rina, almost out of money, was headed back to New York on the Greyhound, then home to England. *Rina.* He ran her name around his mind, feeling its angles, relishing the shapes it would make of his lips when he spoke it.

"Josh said more than a week of California and he'd stagnate."

He kept his face straight as he asked the killer question. "He's your boyfriend?"

"No. We're just friends."

"Stay," he said. His entire face and neck felt ready to melt. "Stay a while longer. My sister's away at Berkeley so there's a spare room at my place. My people would love to meet you."

"Oh it's fine. I'll find a motel. I couldn't just—"

"Sure you could, you're invited! They'd kill me if they knew I hadn't been your Sir Galahad." His voice sounded OK but his eyes were surely betraying him. He put down his coffee cup and stood, to make the idea solidify for all time. There. Decisive.

She stood, too. "All right then. If you're sure?"

And that was it, she said yes, and his feet were moving over the polished floor along with hers, out of Carido's, toward his car… She said yes.

All along the sidewalk his heart rate would not come under enough control for speech, but he had to speak or there'd be a catastrophic silence. "I'm only living with my folks for a short while." He brought off the sentence with only a small gasp, so went for more. "I've just graduated."

And this was *surely* what he'd come back for; that whole stop-start semester was just a chequered path leading right to this moment.

"Oh? What did you do?"

"Fish physiology. It's kind of a branch of marine biology." Sweat sprang to his hairline, but he'd got his credentials in. No need to mention the lack of a proper job yet.

"Hey, that sounds clever! I read about this amazing fish," she said, "the blob fish. It lives at high pressure? Made of jelly and just floats?"

"*Psychrolutes marcidus.* Very high pressures, gelatinous mass rather than muscle. And they're endangered." Stop. Fish nerd. How was that attractive?

"So weird-looking. But cute!"

He stole a glance at her feet, noting the way they shifted in her sandals with each step. Neat toes, each one slightly smaller than the last in the most perfect gradient possible, the nails painted some greeny-blue iridescent color.

"But I suppose all the little kids ask you about blobfish."

They reached his car and Huey grinned. "Ah well, gotta love a weird fish or two!" He steadied his breath as he opened the door for her, but she held his gaze and Smooth-as-Chocolate corpsed. He swallowed. "I hope… that you'll be OK. Our house isn't a mansion or anything…"

"I slept on someone's floor in San Francisco. It'll be luxurious."

Smooth-as-Chocolate rallied again as he drove her away, past the little shop cut right into the bend in the road and the last glimpse of the ocean before the forest swallowed everything, then up on the steep, winding road

21

into the forested hills. And he, Huey, was really doing this.

Didn't she wonder where she might end up? Surely there must be a whit of anxiety. Her expression remained open and calm, as if this was just another in a long line of experiences to devour. She sighed out little comments about how beautiful it would be to live here, and he tried to picture her in some London home. It didn't work. He couldn't place her anywhere, could only see her as something from the ocean.

"Amazing," she said after a mile, "to get so high so quickly. These S-bends are incredible." Her silky hair, forced back onto the headrest by the steep angle of their ascent, flowed into the grooves and tufts of his upholstery. She gazed sideways into the red-lit forest. "And the trees so wide apart. I bet it never gets dark in there till nightfall. I can just imagine those lovely clean needles on the forest floor." She turned to him. "Must be great for picnics?"

Huey nodded.

"No need for a rug, I bet. Oh – do you call them picnics? I keep getting caught out. Do you say barbecue or cook-out?"

"They're interchangeable." His smile – warm, broad – flavored the words with easy drollery. He was doing well, pulling this thing off.

"I love the way you Americans say 'erbs. But scallions – that had me completely baffled. We call them spring onions."

"That's cool. I think I prefer it."

His mother cooed and fussed, transparently charmed by Rina's accent.

"Mom, Dad, this is Rina."

"Rina. What a lovely name! Where does that come from?"

22

"It's Japanese. It means jasmine."

And when she changed for dinner, the mermaid vanished. She wore a silk blouse with wide-legged pants in a sheer, hardly-there fabric. She was perfect. His mom even rustled up a shrimp appetizer. His dad, though, came close to blowing the whole enterprise. "Are you a model?" he asked Rina, catching his ridiculous pinkie ring on Mom's rosebud centerpiece and scattering leaves on Rina's plate.

She laughed. "I'm at college. St Martin's School of Art."

"That right? You're going to be an artist?"

"A graphic designer."

"I knew it. I can see that. You got avant-garde right through you. But you should be a model too. Take it from me."

"*Dad.*" Huey felt a fresh film of sweat forming on his forehead and excused himself. In the bathroom, he ripped off his T-shirt, squirted shower gel onto a sponge and passed it under his arms. He squeezed it out under cool water, reached around and passed it along his back, then splashed his face, changed his T-shirt for an identical dark blue one, and sprayed more deodorant under his arms.

Back at the table, Rina's travels had intoxicated his mother.

"Huey, Rina and her friend did almost the whole of the US together by Greyhound."

"I know, Mom."

"Sausalito's one of her favorite places so far."

His mom placed a hand over Rina's on the table. "We lived in Sausalito when Huey and Amber were tiny. Right around the corner from the waterfront."

"I grew up by the sea. Brighton. My family still live

23

there," Rina said, her accent crisp as crystal against his folks', and Huey pictured both of them landing at Heathrow and making the journey to Brighton, wherever that was. By the sea. Bright and English and green and breezy. Freezing in winter but sharp and invigorating, like that accent—

"American people are so friendly," Rina said. "Josh and I hardy spent any money on motels at all – everyone just invited us home!"

Huey bet Josh didn't get nearly so many invitations now she wasn't with him.

That night he lay in bed reviewing the day, aching for her, imagining her in the room down the hallway, imagining himself creeping in and sliding between her sheets. By the next morning, he knew he had to keep her.

She slept late. Huey paced the porch, determined to dissipate his nervous energy and get the effortless, calm bearing he needed. She'd probably stay with them for at least a week or so, if he played his cards right. So he needed to play it cool and unhurried, no hint of desperation. Girls like to feel you're their friend first and foremost. He'd heard that said so many times.

As soon as she emerged onto the upstairs landing (yawning, tugging hands through her hair), before his parents got to her, he said, "I'll take you for brunch on the boardwalk." Heath Ledger? Almost. "There's a cool seafood place with ocean views."

The next hour passed in a daze of rapturous but nerve-racking delirium. The air seemed crammed with almost insane possibility. Miraculously, she seemed neither bored nor impatient in his company. She smiled in the doorway of the boardwalk restaurant. She smiled at the menu, at the interior, at Huey. We get along, Huey thought again, electrified. This is how it feels when it's right.

24

He tried to focus on the places she told him she'd visited, but could think of nothing but her clear steady gaze as she read, the way her long fingers balanced the menu, the way her hair looped and spread over her bare arms.

"I'm going to travel, too," he said, fearless, floating. "Next year we could do Europe together. Agreed?"

It felt like a foregone conclusion and Rina accepted it with light laughter, just as she accepted most things he said. He began to construct a family of people who looked like her. He added a trail blazed through London's landmarks, Japanese food eaten on a riverboat with all those iconic bridges threaded through each other in the background.

"I can picture you in Istria," she said. "Red-roofed beach towns, mountains—"

"Hey, Huey! What are you *doing* here?" Erin had arrived from nowhere. Her eyes moved between Huey and Rina; quizzical amusement played around her mouth.

"Oh, Rina, this is my friend Erin. Erin, Rina." He stood and maneuvered between the two women like he'd seen people do, but his voice rose higher as the introduction went on and became a shambles. "We were in high school together." A colossal amount of heat flooded his face as he sat down again. Erin might just as well have brought a furnace to their table.

"Great to meet you, Rina." As usual, Erin was making herself at home. She carried foaming coffee in a very small cup, as if she'd been behind the counter and helped herself. She turned to Rina. "Have Huey bring you by later."

"I'm working this afternoon," Huey said.

Erin and Rina made eye contact, and Erin raised one thinly plucked eyebrow. Only last year she'd been more of

25

a cashmere-and-micro-skirt girl, but now her Goth phase was fully loaded. Her hair was jet black and the blonde regrowth could be mistaken for bald strips. Her face was now so pale, she looked like a penguin chick with a ferocious determination.

"Better yet, she can come while you're at work, then she won't have to be bored." Erin smiled at Rina and wrinkled her nose. "It's the Espirit Coffee House. Have him drop you off."

Erin sauntered away and a wave of bacon aroma filled the gap she left.

Rina looked at him and tilted her head forward. "I get the feeling you're less than keen?"

"Oh, that crowd, you know. I was in high school with them, but we don't have that much in common anymore." She didn't comment, just smiled kindly, so Huey felt able to go on, focusing on the curve of her neck, then her eyes, up, down, up again. "Ah, you know... they're in the Cool crowd. And I'm not." He pulled a face and she giggled. "So, like, I don't have piercings, I don't have tattoos. I'm not into drugs – they just don't interest me. Is that a crime?"

She laughed and shook her head. "I know."

"I brought you here for brunch, and to them this is totally the most uncool place to hang out. They would have brought you to a shit-hole downtown, just because it served the most Mexican food and had the loudest music."

Rina nodded, still grinning.

"I love fish, and they could care less. I even love the itty bitty nth degree of what goes on in their cells..."

"But you must have had friends at uni who loved that too."

He blinked several times. "Not osmoregulation. Na-ah."

"What?"

"Osmoregulation. It's how creatures stop their cells from getting too diluted or too concentrated. We all do it, but I got into how fish do it especially." He watched her reaction, looking for signs of boredom or amusement. "I just got into the smallest stuff in a big way. Smaller and smaller."

She looked at him, clearly fascinated. But was it good fascination or bad?

"Smaller and smaller," she said. "I once knew somebody who loved the number zero, and he wasn't even a mathematician. I know how these things can be." She continued to study him, as if something invisible blocked her view. "So that's what you're going to do, eventually?"

"Yup. I'm only working at the bar until…"

She put her cup down and leaned forward. He could almost breathe in her exhaled air.

"…well, you know, my plan was to come home and do research at UCLA or work hands-on at IMS in Santa Cruz. Sorry – that's the Institute of Marine Sciences. But, you know, that's kind of what everyone thinks, I guess." He mimed putting a gun to his head and pulling the trigger.

"Oh, but you should carry on trying to do what you love. Definitely. You'll find a way." She put a hand on his knee for an instant. "And you're a scientist! That's a fantastic achievement."

Huey nodded, burning at her touch, wanting it back, his mind creating a dizzying flash of her as the mermaid who exchanged legs for a tail, and then her phone buzzed. She giggled, read the text, tapped in her reply.

"Sorry. It's from Josh. He says he's met a new friend, but he's spelt it 'fiend'." She giggled again.

"Tell him you hope his new fiend doesn't eat him," Huey said.

Rina put her phone in her bag and patted it with, Huey deduced, an air of finality. She pressed her pastry with the flat of her knife. Huey watched steam rise from the crumbs, smelt hot apple as she said, "What's the coffee house like?"

Huey hesitated; an air of stillness hung about her, as if she waited for something more than his answer. "People sprawl on old leather couches and read papers and talk about books and music. It's what you would expect with that crowd. It's cool. But you have to be ready to talk about Nietzsche and have your hair way freaked."

She laughed, said it sounded like it might be fun, so after driving home to get ready for work, he took her and left her there, on the brink of telling her how he felt every step of the journey. How should he word it? Or should he just kiss her? Best not. That could come off as a lunge. He'd frighten her away. Words were probably better.

Rina had exchanged her floaty dress for skinny jeans and vest, as if she'd joined the coffee house crowd already. Huey tightened inside. So, she could metamorphose. That ability made her even more appealing.

It wasn't late by the time Huey finished work and made it to the coffee house, but the moon hung big and yellow over the water. If people could even see all the fish beneath it... No, if he could *show* the world those fish, make everyone really see them in the way he did, make them know what he knew. The real poetry in the world lay in those cells, and with Rina, he might just come close to—

Rina sat with Lawrence on a low cream leather

couch that seated two.

"The back-story is awesome," Lawrence was saying, "It's like they totally raided my head. Shit."

Although Rina smiled a hello at Huey, she remained next to Lawrence, the Heidegger of the day. Huey's stomach felt gassy. It bubbled. It was hard not to match the bubbling with the rhythm of the 1940s Jazz on the coffee house sound system.

Huey opened his mouth. "So... coffee smooth enough tonight, guys?" He cringed as soon as the words were out. If only he could find that perfect opening line, make everything seem easy and mellow, especially in front of Lawrence, who'd poke even the tiniest chink. He felt large and conspicuous beside Lawrence's rangy, folded-daddy-long-legs frame; dough-faced next to Lawrence's angular features, Lawrence's bookish stubble, Lawrence's calico shirt in just the right shade of clay.

Rina smiled at Huey again, but didn't seem to think she needed to say anything, so Lawrence poured on in his intense, flat voice.

Huey sucked in a long breath. He was going to have to make a move, stake his claim, but heat radiated up from his neck, and his shirt stuck to his back. If things did work out and she passed her hands across his body, they'd come off wet. So he sweated through the crowd to the bathroom and sorted himself out.

Later, the whole coffee house drifted back to Lawrence's house and somehow, on the way, Rina must have snorted something. It was obvious. It pulsed out in her expansive attitude, the glaze in her eyes as she stood in the kitchen making food with Erin, emptying packets of chips into bowls, laughing at something he didn't understand. He went back to the den and downed a beer quickly. Need to get with this program, he thought, but when he went back to the kitchen, she had gone.

He found her in the hallway at the bottom of the stairs, standing in a position that was neither particularly noticeable nor downright hidden. He blinked once: definitely Rina. He could see her hair, Lawrence's hands twining in it as they kissed. He stood in the doorway. Their shadows were huge and gothic on the floor; it could have been straight from a movie. He didn't linger, but saw enough to recognize the hunger in her: she returned the kiss like she'd been starving.

But I found her, he thought. I fucking found her.

Back in the main room, noise hummed around him. Doors opened and slammed closed; people came and went, some held hands, others performed parodies of dances to music that was an insult to him now. A face flashed before him, flushed pink in the dim light, sleek headed, long haired – no. A stranger.

Smoke drifted in from outside and mixed with the smell of hot bodies, yet he didn't go home. He couldn't leave her here.

Later still, when Rina and Lawrence had disappeared upstairs, as he leaned against the door frame staring out at the distant ocean, Erin floated by, jangling her arm bangles. "You look thunderous. I didn't know you had that in you."

He stayed silent. A burst of cool air bathed his face, but he kept his eyes on the saltmarsh channels Lawrence so thoughtlessly walked past every day.

"Don't do it to yourself, Huey."

I can't help it, he thought. That's why it's called *falling* in love.

She slapped his back. "Chalk this one up to experience."

Even later, when Huey was much drunker, Erin found him again, still leaning, still staring.

"Huey," she said, her voice sing-song, her expression concerned. "The ship has gone down, taking all hands." She flicked a dead match into the night and Huey listened to it bounce down the porch steps. "Time to sail on."

"But I found her. I found her on the beach."

Erin shook her head. Keeping her eyes on Huey, she walked backwards, slowly, to the kitchen door. "My grandma used to say, 'Never keep anything you find on the beach. You don't know where it's been'."

That was the last thing he heard before he shouldered through the bodies and crashed on the floor behind the couch. In his dreams, he wasn't on the floor. He was back at home and so was Rina. He floated out of his room and into hers, into her, all night, and for the rest of their lives.

Rina and Huey shuffled home at dawn. Rina must have crashed, too, with her lover in some bedroom. He could let her know he'd seen the kiss, stare this whole thing down. Or he could vow never to let her know. He played with the words in his head: *vow never to let her know.* It sounded like something Lawrence might say.

"Uh, we're going to have to walk to the cab stand – I can't risk driving." His voice sounded gruff. He could say what he thought out loud. He could say, *Love is not love which alters when it alteration finds.* Maybe he could stop doing what he always did and perhaps get a different result. So he said, "I didn't know Lawrence'd split with his girlfriend." He'd fought hard for the words to come out without petulance, and now his mouth tasted of metal.

31

"Nope. She's back next week." There was a pause. Their steps synchronized and he couldn't work out how: who accommodated whom? "I know," Rina went on, "we did a bad thing." She shrugged, as if none of it mattered and she was just an avatar in her own adventure.

The breath leaving his nostrils felt like steam. "Did he tell you about her before, during or after?"

Her eyes were downcast now, watching the road pass beneath their feet, as if concentrating on the dark grey of it, like a child. She didn't answer, and in so doing, blunted his sarcasm.

They had to walk around a crouching dog about to crap on the pavement, its owner looking almost as wrecked as the two of them. It should have been funny. Huey sneaked a sidelong glance at Rina to see if she'd even noticed. Her hair no longer fell sleekly and un-knotted all over. Wavy tendrils stuck to her forehead and the sides of her face, and he felt his desire for her quilt over, as if crocheted by a fervent old aunt.

Neither of them spoke as the road opened out at the Firth intersection, where the whole peninsular came into view. A gust blew Rina's hair into her eyes, then went on to lift the lightest branches of some top-heavy bush leaning into their path. It would have been one of the most beautiful sunrises ever if his throbbing head had let his eyes see it properly. It might have been a dream-like déjà-vu mind trick brought on by his hangover, but he knew he'd always remember walking back with her, that every brick and branch and tree would record it.

"Oh my God," Rina said. "My bloody head is starting. I thought I'd got away with it, but no – here it comes."

"Uh-huh."

And now, as he relaxed into it, the rest of their

32

journey passed with surprising ease. A cab waited at Monroe's corner. The ride should have been awkward, but it was nothing; there was peace in this emptiness. He looked out at the ocean, imagined a bony fish deep down, maintaining equilibrium with its environment. Sometimes he could almost feel himself doing it, too.

Huey woke to light slanting through his bedroom blinds at a strange angle. Then his head cleared. It was 2pm: afternoon sunlight. The very particular, familiar noise outside his door that had featured in his dreams started up again. Someone was walking back and forth between the bathroom and one of the bedrooms.

Downstairs in the hall, Rina's backpack sat by the front door, propped against his old camera tripod case. In the kitchen, in front of his mom where protest was impossible, she said, "Listen, you've all been so lovely, but I should really be making tracks now."

Huey squeezed the hem of his T-shirt with one hand. He stayed in the kitchen doorway and stared at a stain on the floor, trying to make his mind close off. His breath seemed hardly there anyway.

Driving Rina to the bus station began badly. It was like driving through thickened air, air that had been doused with glue.

"So beautiful," Rina said as they passed through the redwoods. "Their height alone sends you into a rapture, doesn't it?"

Huey's hands on the steering wheel were dry. "Yeah." He knew he sounded jaded, but he could remember balancing the front tire of his bike off the ridge of that huge tree root right there, when he was about fourteen.

And then he felt the whole weekend wash over him

and roll away, like a wave turning back to the ocean. She made easy, constant small talk anyway. She'd go back via Albuquerque, just because of the name. And there was St. Louis, and New Orleans: riches beyond dreams, even if she could only afford to pass right through. *Beautiful.* She used the word again and yet again. He had a feeling that no matter what he said, no matter his demeanor, she'd carry on with this warm, polite banter. She'd take it right through her life, use it in every situation.

He put her on the Greyhound. He did it physically: guiding her by the elbow, handing her the backpack, standing on the step with her while they hugged, kissed on the lips, laughed and smiled wide, eye-crinkling grins at each other.

"You'd better call," he murmured into her ear, knowing he must savor the smell of her hair – flowery, fresh – the softness of her skin as they brushed cheeks.

"I will! Soon!"

He knew she wouldn't, knew she'd said those words all over the States.

"We'll do Europe!" he shouted up at her window. She nodded. He nodded back and gave her a big smile. His best.

About the author
Clare Weze is a biologist currently dividing her time between editing scientific publications and writing fiction. In 2012 her book *The House of Ash* was shortlisted for the Commonword Children's Diversity Writing Prize, and her short fiction has appeared in several anthologies. She lives in North Yorkshire.

Angels

Sally Angell

The receiver fell from Ruth's hand, a voice at the other end going faint and scribbly. But she knew. And she wasn't ready. How could anyone ever be ready? It was too much. Her senses struggled for the tools learnt to cope with stress. Ruth looked up. Waited. No warmth. No comfort. Nothing.

Standing in the surreal brightness of the coffee shop on the designated day, she still isn't ready. The thick buttoned coat and neck-hugging scarf don't stop her shivering. The future has become one of those fiction stories with different conclusions, where the reader decides the one they want. But she, Ruth Simmonds, won't be able to write hers.

At a table in the far corner Tara's back is hunched and unmoving, her half-brushed hair sticking up at the collar of the fleece she seems to live in. Ruth's stomach flips. Tara shouldn't be caught up in all this. Twenty-six is a time for enjoying youth, or at least being free to explore possibilities. A mother isn't her daughter's responsibility, but there's no one else locally. And Ruth badly needs someone with her today.

Copies of a new poster are stuck up on the walls of the coffee house. It's a festive offer. There's a digital picture, a bowl with steam zig-zagging up above it. 'Coming soon! 1st December – Christingal Special – Delicious Hot Soup with Roast Potatos, Turkey, Chipolata and Vegtable pieces.' She can't produce the critical grimace that would be automatic for Normal Ruth. Her hands are stiff too, as if the fingers belong to someone else, when she tries to count change for the till.

What's the point? The mantra has returned, like text

that should be deleted but keeps running on, printing over and over in her mind. But it's vital to keep functioning. One move at a time. Select sachets of sugar, teaspoons, paper napkins. Tea sludges over as Ruth raises her arms over buggies and shoppers' paraphernalia, and bumps the tray down at Tara's elbow.

"Blueberry muffin," she manages. "And one hot chocolate." The black-lined rims of eyes that are a younger version of her own are zombie-blank. A nonspeaking day then apart from the earlier outburst in the queue.

Embarrassment prickles Ruth's neck now at the humiliation. It was their turn to order. Tara was rigid and hostile beside her. Short-fused, Ruth heard herself shout, "Will you – will you – FLAMING WELL make up your mind!" A buzzing started, and she realized it was inside her head. How could she? How *could* she lose it with the one person who'd stuck with her all through the nightmare so far?

"Shut up!" Tara's head had jerked back in panic as if she wanted to be anywhere else but here. And who could blame her? People were looking, looking away, and Ruth knew what they were thinking. They were thinking she was a monster. A Monster Mother.

This fruit scone's off. She could be chewing cardboard. Tea. The steaming liquid burns her stomach. And her brain goes all high and tingly, which could be another symptom. Any bodily sensation is a worry. Like the spasms that spark in her chest, that must be something.

A woman in the yellow *Mugs* overall is crashing used trays and trash onto her trolley. Refilling the cutlery holders at the time, she was a witness to the great mother/daughter meltdown. Her eyes don't move as she passes their table. *She doesn't know*, Ruth reminds herself. No one does. The enormity, the loneliness and terror of

36

what she is going through is incomprehensible to anyone else, unless they've been there. It is beyond cruel. Just as she has finally let go of fear and allowed a fragile trust, the dreaded word has come.

'Recall'.

Ruth casts round for something, anything to distract her thoughts. To give relief. The turkey image underneath the bowl, on the soup poster, has a smiley face. And it gets her. Like a switch, the world is right again and not the parallel one she's been relegated to for so long, like a child shut out from a party pressing its face to the window. It happens sometimes, a rewind to Before. Normality. A lightness of spirit. Joy even. Ruth blocks out the message on the phone. Stay positive.

In this flow of this energy she reaches out, touches the fraying navy sleeve, and pulls a face up at the poster. Silly stupid turkey doesn't realize he's oven ready! And the spelling! Usually they'd roll their eyes at that, she and Tara together. But one fleeced arm bends up defensively, in front of this face that Ruth loves most in the world; this face that has no colour, that doesn't look like the face of her daughter. Ruth wants to wipe away the smudge of hot chocolate moustache on it as gut fear hits her, that fear a mother feels for her child's vulnerability. Especially now, with life gone bum over belly as Tara would say, if she was feeling herself.

Ruth sees not the young adult before her, but the little girl who needed to be wrapped up warm against the cold. And the outside temperature today is arctic, enough to freeze your bits off. The hang of sky out of the smeary window is a dark painful swell as it holds onto its burden. Not so in other regions of the country. The glittering landscape up north, forecast last night, is the photograph

37

on the front page of the daily paper Ruth grabbed from Smith's, along with a mixture of magazines. In case they have to wait at the clinic. In the middle counties, too, snowfall has rubbed out roads and islanded cars. Not here though. Not yet. There's just the clamp of winter's hand like an unwanted presence.

Tara stands up clumsily, and for a moment Ruth thinks she's going to leave her. But it's the cake cabinet she's after. Ruth clicks her phone on. One more hour to go. The interior of *Mugs* is dotted with slumped figures, escaping from homes they can't afford to heat, to glean a little comfort from the lighted shopfronts, perhaps imbibe some human warmth. Too early for Christmas, November is a malady to get through. If only, for herself, it could just be that; the nameless gloom of winter. The longing makes her ache. If only.

She visualizes how the garden looked this morning, how she'd tried not to look in case she saw that unnatural, too glittery sharpness of the bare trees, remembered from last time.

"Children, eh?" The trolley woman is back, whisking away the empty plates and rubbish from their table. "You can't do wrong for doing right!" Her appearance goes from grey and unfriendly to bright and kind, someone on Ruth's side.

Tara's back, looking better now, a pinkness creeping under her skin. "That old guy who moved in next door," she says. Ruth blinks. Tara sits down and starts to pick the chocolate chips from her muffin. "He was sweeping leaves on his patio when I called round yours. That day you were out. He asked me in for coffee."

An adult Tara might be, but Ruth's instincts kick in as if she's still six. You warn them and protect them, and teach them to look after themselves. But some harms, new and terrible and beyond anyone's understanding, just happen anyway.

Tara nods. "I think he fancies you."

They're kind now at the local hospital, the staff. They have to be. It's all they've got. The report from the recent inspection said all the medical services required improvement.

It's like the Caribbean in here, after outside. Ruth didn't want to risk the bus not turning up, so they have walked up from the coffee shop in town. Ruth uses the hand gel before they go through the swing doors. This is like one of those dramas which keeps showing flashbacks to update the story for viewers. She's treading the same corridors she walked before, recognizing smells, being shown to the same row of chairs.

There may be a wait," the Healthcare Assistant says. "We're very busy today."

Well you will be, Ruth wants to retort. An appointment was arranged, Ruth psyched herself up to go for a further test after the yearly check she has to have now. Something they wanted to take a closer look at.

Another call. "Our systems are down. The machines aren't working." And so there has been another four days of waiting, god-bargaining, chanting positive affirmations and playing meditation CDs. Of presences.

"Do you talk to the angels, Ruth?" the therapy girl had asked, one afternoon as she poured almond oil into a dish. She looked normal, this Melissa who had been in the folder at the library, and Ruth thought yes, that's what I need, deep, deep relaxation. Melissa seemed quite practically-minded, as a teacher at reputable venues. All the treatments she offered were printed out on her business card; Indian Head Massage, Reiki, Affirmations,

EFT, Hypnotherapy, reflexology. She did home visits. And she was a healer; it was in her family.

But now she was going on about angels. How to reply? Ruth hadn't wanted to upset her, but didn't like to lie.

"It seems – a dumbing down of religion. Like – like – classroom assistants instead of teachers."

Melissa's laugh was gentle, as she dropped essential oils into the dish. Lavender, frankincense, geranium. Bergamot was lovely. Just a few drops with the base oil, a sensual instant garden.

"The angels were created by God, and they do his work." She dipped her fingers into the warm oils, and began to work them deeply into Ruth's tormented shoulders.

When she first had the massages her body screamed resentment at the harshness on her cranium, after the weeks of constant physical trauma, all the pain and the loss of the surgery. But it became easier over time, and uplifting, like having her nails done or her hair.

"Michael is the angel for safety and technical problems," Melissa's soft voice continued. "Raphael is for health." She would lend Ruth a book she promised, which would tell her what they all did.

"I kept an angel pin on my locker when I had the operation." Ruth had forgotten. The brooch, a girl shape in a pink dress had been a present from a relative from abroad for Christmas that year. Just a cheap glass trinket. But it was something to hold in her palm before being wheeled off on the trolley to have a body part severed, which, she realized in the aftermath had chillingly become almost normalized that year. Like dentists' current policy to do extractions rather than repairs. Yes, that one's got to be removed, and that one, and that one.

"Ms Simmonds. Would you come through." Ruth gulps, grimaces at Tara and follows the girl in the pale blue uniform. She takes a basket as instructed. She knows the ritual. Remove all your top clothing. Put the gown on. Then go and sit in the waiting room.

"I've been here ages," the woman on the plastic chair next to hers says. "I've read all the copies of *Hello*. Is it snowing yet?"

"No." Ruth says. "Not when we came in."

Neither her own magazines, nor the ones here make any sense to her. The words are like a foreign language. As she puts the pile back down on the coffee table, something glints near one of the wooden legs. Twenty pence. A coin! Melissa would say it's a sign; that your angels are with you.

"I'm getting the name," Melissa's hand hovered over her head at one of their sessions, and a lovely indigo light flowed between Ruth's eyes, "of your guardian angel. Yes, it's – Ria."

"We're ready for you now." The voice brings her back. Ruth breathes in deeply. Trust. Oh, help me, guardian angel! She carries her basket into the side room.

"At least I've had five more years." Ruth's babbling on to Tara. She's back in the main waiting area. A doctor has looked at the images, and she has to have an ultrasound. It's all wrong. This sort of test has always been for when women have babies, the healthy creation of life. Now it's a probe to find bad stuff that shouldn't be there.

It had been a white January back then when it all began, shock followed by a relentless process. In that hospital room she'd fumbled over to the window, released the blinds to a black night and the ghostly car park below. The vehicles were mounds, and the white hard cap on each roof reminded her of mountains and the coldly clinical air of high altitudes that can stop breath. Mountains like Kilimanjaro where women would climb

41

that year to raise money. Brave women, damaged women like herself, but who still had fire at their core, that defiance of extinction.

How can she go through it all again? So disruptive and difficult. And what's going to happen to Tara? She's not in a good place either. First the break up with her partner, then only just hanging on to the flat. She doesn't see friends, or go anywhere. And now she'll be checking herself constantly. It's a worry.

There's a side door to the right of the waiting area. Ruth's feet propel her towards it and then she's through and outside, gasping freezing oxygen into her lungs. The sky, the clouds, the air itself, are swollen. Surely, surely, now it will snow.

Her name's called from inside, and it's like she's in some Hitchcock movie where reality is impossible. In the treatment room she can't move. They have to push her into position. Kind voices. Jelly on her skin. The cold instrument presses on skin, veins, tissue, invading this most sensitive area of the body.

Blue light, says the voice inside her, blue light, the colour of love, is absorbed into every cell of your body. She shuts her eyes. Michael please keep me safe. God, help me. And the shining, shining yellow rays, the warm golden light of healing. Raphael, heal me. But all the while the pressing and pain. It's not their fault, she thinks, dully, that something's wrong.

Ruth takes the cup of tea and sips it gratefully. It doesn't seem like two weeks since that awful day. Tara calls round most mornings. She's had her hair styled, Ruth notices, and has put on make-up. She's wearing a coat today and boots, and the dead look has gone from her eyes. As Tara leaves, she says she's meeting friends in town. Ruth takes the tea upstairs.

A tap from below makes her panicky; the front door. She looks down at the three-nights-old pyjamas, with a stain down the jacket front. Keeps still and quiet. The letter box jiggles. Perhaps it's an early Christmas card delivered by hand.

Ruth edges to the window. Someone's still there. The top of a head is visible. The figure stands back and looks up. She pulls back quickly. She lets three minutes tick by on the clock, and then creeps down to see what's there.

A small card lies on the mat. "If you need anything, contact me. Bob." There's the address and phone number. His name is printed underneath. Robert Ian Andrews.

Ruth stares at the initials. She starts to laugh, and can hear other laughter all around her. She opens the door and feels the chill through her socks and slippers as she steps out and calls after the man from next door. He spins round, squinting through the morning sun. He's not that old. Ruth wonders what it would be like to be held again. There is more of life's story to unfold.

She remembers the pressure stopping, and the doctor's voice. That's it. You're all right. Her disbelief. What? Then she was asking the nurse over and over, "He did say, did he say I'm OK?"

Yes. A smile. You are all right.

The air lightens. Ruth lifts her head, feels a feather touch. The first snowflake.

About the author

Sally Angell loves literature and writing, and is always aiming to develop new and original ideas in her work. Sally explores the truth and reality of feelings, the originality of language and the possibilities of words. She likes to write stories with contemporary themes, that also have a universal meaning. Her writing has been published in magazines and anthologies.

Natural Recycle

Derek Corbett

Lifting his old baseball cap, Cramps combed back his long white straggly hair with his fingers and sat down on a tree stump. Taking out a tin holding his cigarette makings from the, patched pocket of his dirty grey threadbare overcoat, he removed the lid. The tobacco, a blend of other people's discarded quality dog ends, he called 'Recycle', named after hearing about the subject from other travellers like himself.

The subject fascinated him so much, he would pass the time as he walked the roads, dreaming up ways of using the discarded items he passed. Unlike some of his fellow travellers however, he never picked the items up, he'd seen too many of them struggling with their wobbly-wheeled supermarket trolleys, to be slowed down by unwanted baggage.

Removing a packet of cigarette papers from the half full tin and pulling out a single sheet, he hung it from his lip, before taking just the right amount of tobacco. Shop bought, the papers provided a better smoke than newspaper and anyway they were recycled paper.

Pausing for a moment to enjoy the smell of the orange peel he used to keep his tobacco moist, he returned the pack of papers, replaced the lid and dropped it back in his pocket. Spreading the shredded leaf along the delicate thin white strip he rolled the paper around the loosely packed tobacco with his stiff dirt-grimed fingers, wet the gum and gave it a final roll before twisting the end.

The making was always the same, the same actions carried out in the same order, a ritual. He had done it the same way for years, ever since a strong wind had lifted the contents of his tin, spreading them out across the countryside; he'd been three days without a smoke after that little episode.

Placing the cigarette between wind chapped lips, Cramps took a 'throw away' lighter from his pocket. Recovered after spotting its previous owner doing exactly what its name implied, he rubbed it between the palms of his hands to vaporise the dregs, before cupping the end of the cigarette with his hand and striking the flint.

Waiting until the flaming twisted paper had gone out, Cramps took a draw followed by a short pause, before a coughing spasm announced the lungs attempt to reject their first alien intake of the day.

"See you're still keeping up with the morning exercises."

Finishing the bout of coughing, Cramps spat to one side and wiped his mouth with the back of his hand, before turning to look disdainfully at the little old man now sitting beside him.

Eighteen inches high, with long straggling white hair partly controlled by an old baseball cap, he also wore the same dirty threadbare grey overcoat as himself. On his face an all knowing smile or as Cramps called it, a 'smirk'.

"I knew you'd be around as soon as I was out of the town," growled the old tramp.

"You know I don't like all that noise and foul air, anyway there's too much distraction, at least out here I get some of your attention."

"And why would you want my attention?" asked Cramps taking another draw of the hot smoke.

"Well nobody else is going to talk to you are they, not from choice anyway."

"What do you mean, lots of people talk to me."

"Yeah, but only to move you on."

"Anyway how would you know, you're never there," snapped Cramps sliding a hand inside his coat to rub his sore chest.

"Of course I am, it's just that you can't see me, but I know you can still hear me, and anyway I don't have a choice but to be with you."

"Choice....course you've got a choice; everyone's got a choice," exclaimed Cramps.

"So why do you live like you do?" asked the little man.

"There you go again implying that there's something wrong with being a 'gentleman of the Highways', don't you ever give up?"

"Gentleman, ha!" laughed the little man sarcastically, "you fancy yourself a gentleman, you can't even spell it?"

Cramps let out a long groan.

"And you always have to bring that up too, don't you."

"What, the fact that you can't read or write? What's wrong with talking about it, you had the choice to learn when you were young, you chose not to."

"No I didn't choose not to learn, I just decided that I didn't like being 'learned' in a class room, by bored and boring Teachers."

"You're beginning to sound a little defensive, have I hit a sore spot perhaps?"

Cramps let out another sigh and turned his back on the little man before taking another draw of his roll-up.

How could I afford to miss all this by being stuck in a rotten classroom he thought as he followed the line of hedgerows across the countryside.

Finishing his smoke and dropping the dog-end Cramps stood up and ground it out with his string-tied well-worn boot before picking up his plastic-covered rope-bound bundle.

"Where we off to?" enquired the little man.

Ignoring the question Cramps took his first step.

Somewhere between a conventional step and a sliding forward goosestep of his bad leg, the result of being hit by a truck years before, he called it his 'highway' shuffle.

"Not really sure but I know it's in this direction."

"Hasn't it got a name or are you keeping it a secret?"

"Yes," said Cramps, a smile showing at the edges of his mouth, knowing his answer would be annoying.

"What do you want to go 'there' for?"

"Because," answered Cramps enjoying the moment.

"But you always go 'there' this time of the year."

Cramps bit his lip so as not to laugh at the little man's attempt to find out where he was heading.

"And why not, it's a very beautiful place," replied Cramps, suddenly noticing for the first time the little man's funny walk, somewhere between a conventional step and a sliding forward goosestep of his bad leg.

"But don't you fancy somewhere different for a change?"

"Not really, it's nice to revisit places and recall old memories."

"You mean like 'recycling' experiences?" suggested the little man.

"Exactly."

Having shuffled their way through the deserted high street of a tiny village the little man spoke again.

"Do you know that's only the second time that I can recall, you've ever actually agreed with something I've said, in all these years."

"When was the first then?"

"That time you got caught out on the moors in a snow storm and thought you were going to die."

"And what did we agree on?" asked Cramps, trying hard to ignore the pain in his chest.

"That maybe, just maybe, you should have chosen a different way of living."

"Oh yeah, I remember… but I also remember that just afterwards I decided that I had made the right choice."

"Was that before or after the AA man found you half frozen to death under that bush?"

The old tramp looked ahead into the distance rubbing at the pain; he knew he was getting close to where he had to go, he could sense it.

"Before… just before," he answered thoughtfully.

Continuing in silence, the yearning for the familiar sights driving him on, his chest pain was now almost constant. His legs, not good at the best of times, felt as if they were about to collapse under him.

For two pins I'd sit down right now, if it wasn't so close and anyway the little bloke would only start annoying me again.

"How we doing?" asked the little man.

"It's better when you don't bug me?" replied Cramps gritting his teeth against the pain.

"Not for much longer I shouldn't wonder," added the little man knowingly.

Cramps reached the top of the long hill and turned off the lane into woods to follow a familiar path between the tall trees.

"Isn't it peaceful in here?" declared the Tramp.

"But we've not heard a sound for the last hour, the road's been empty."

"But this is different, and anyway I said peaceful, not quiet."

"I know where we're going," announced the little man suddenly. "This leads to that spot that overlooks a valley where a river runs from one end to the other."

Stumbling, Cramps put out his hand to steady himself against the trunk of a tree, the feel of its bark somehow so familiar, yet he knew he'd never touched that particular tree before. Pushing himself upright he continued walking unsteadily on the thick carpet of last year's leaves.

"What happens to all these leaves?" asked the little man, kicking a few into the air.

"They rot away into the ground to become food for the trees so that they can grow yet more leaves."

"Sounds a bit like your stupid recycle thing."

"No 'sort of' about it, 'Recycling' is exactly what it is, in fact probably the greatest example of recycling there is," snapped Cramps, grabbing again at his chest.

Coming to the edge of the woods he sat down on a fallen tree, a victim of last year's high winds.

"You're crabby this morning."

"So would you be if you had someone 'rabbiting' in your ear all the time about why you didn't make this or that choice," complained Cramps. Falling silent he began to follow the winding river marvelling at how the sun was reflecting off its surface.

It's like silver thread, he thought, *a silver thread laid across the countryside. I wonder if anyone has ever described it that way in a book?*

"If you'd learned to read you might have found the answer to that question," exclaimed the little man.

"Taken to reading my thoughts now have you?" croaked Cramps as another much stronger pain hit him in the chest. "I'll be glad when you're gone."

"And I'll be glad when you're gone," retorted the little man angrily. "Then you can become part of that

49

stupid recycle thing you keep harping on about. Probably finish up as one of those leaves I shouldn't wonder."

"That wouldn't be such a bad thing," replied Cramps calmly.

"Bloody silly if you ask me."

Cramps turned quickly–to look at the little man. "That's your problem, isn't it? That's why you've hounded me all these years, you're jealous, because when I go it's all over for you. You have never been able to enjoy the wonder of being alive, you can never be recycled, never be a part of the great magnificent on-going scheme of things. You're just so much excess baggage I've acquired over the years, which in the end amounts to nothing."

Cramps watched as the enraged little man opened his mouth to say something, but instead, slowly faded from sight. Sighing with relief the Tramp took out his tobacco tin and opened it.

"I wouldn't have missed any of this for the world," he said out loud beginning the ritual of rolling a cigarette while again following the flow of the river. Another pain, he could tell would be a bad one, began to grow in his chest. Steeling himself expectantly the pain suddenly stopped allowing him to relax. Dropping his tin, the contents spilled to drift out across the valley as he slumped along the tree trunk. Cramps had become a part of the greatest recycle process of them all…Mother Nature.

About the author

A retired Engineer from the Petro-Chemical Industry, Derek's first attempt at writing a short story was in 1982 while working in Norway. Returning to UK in 1984 he joined a writing club entering only club competitions until retiring in 2004. Since then he has submitted without success a few short stories to magazines and the occasional competition. He has also been a member of a monthly Critique group since 2011.

Winter Scenes

Margaret Bulleyment

Today, there's ten of them. But which one is it? Boho cardigan middle-aged lady? Pixie boot student? Leather jacket guy? Who is it and what am I going to do, when I find out?

Winter Mystery Tour Lady
c/o Ashmolean Museum
Beaumont St
Oxford OX1 2PH

Thursday Nov 6

Dear 'Miss Snowflake'? (Sarah? Susan? Sorry, I did not quite catch your name, but I know it began with an 'S'.)

I wanted to let you know how much I enjoyed your Mystery Art Tour yesterday. It was fun just showing up and not knowing what the theme was, never mind what I was actually going to see. And what gems those Konstantin Korovin (spelling?) paintings are!!!!! I'd never heard of him and just thought that Impressionists were French, painting in all that light and sun, down south. Who would have thought that Russian winter scenes were in the same movement?

What a great idea to show people hidden corners of the galleries, rather than just the most famous stuff and I bet you enjoy it more than giving yet another talk on Uccello, or the Alfred Jewel.

Keep up the good work.
Winter Tour Lover

That was the first time anyone had written to thank me for a tour. A proper letter even, written by someone who sounded as though they had a good sense of humour. I found it in my pigeonhole, along with all the usual mundane missives and email printouts and it made my day. I took it home and showed it to Mum, like a toddler with her first finger painting.

"Winter Tour Lover is quite right," she said, when she had finished reading it. "After all, the tours were your idea and they've been very successful. And it's to John Stevens's credit, that he has so much faith in his younger members of staff, that he follows up their ideas."

The Head of the Education Department just happens to be a friend of Mum's, but I like to think I got my position on my own merits. I can at least copy the letter so he sees it and perhaps, we can use the beginning of the second paragraph, in our publicity shots.

Thursday Nov 13

Dear Sarah, (I listened harder this time)
Another enjoyable Winter Tour, yesterday. Yes, I know I could have done a different tour on another day, with someone else, but I wanted to hear you again and catch the bits I missed last week.

It was good that parts of it were different this time – you obviously don't just repeat yourself parrot-fashion. The fact that the paintings are some of your own favourites, came over very well. It was interesting that someone who sounds so British, was born in California and I loved the description of you aged five in this country, seeing snow for the first time and trying to eat it. That must be why you like winter scenes so much. I do too.

Our friend Korovin, would have taken snow for granted where he came from, although the little figures all by themselves in the middle of his paintings, look like they're struggling a bit. When it snows in Russia, it really snows – not so much snow games, more like survival games.

Best Wishes
Winter Tour Lover

I never noticed the same person on this week's *Winter Tour*, but then people come and go all the time and unless someone asks you a question, you really don't notice them. I told Mum the Winter Tour Lover had come again, but I didn't show her the letter this time, as it somehow seemed more personal.

Thursday Nov 20

Dear Sarah,
Now, I really feel I am getting to know you and Korovin. It registered this time that he painted dozens of those scenes just to make money, when his Parisian dreams did not turn out quite like he imagined they would. Life never does, does it? If you're hankering after the snows of your native land, Paris is probably not as warm and friendly as it might first appear. (There's a joke in that sentence somewhere.)
I looked up more Korovin paintings on the internet (you've got me really interested) and the Parisian ones, I think, look a bit hollow. The Russian winter scenes may not be his greatest paintings, but at least they feel real. They show us

who he is and we all like to know who we are, don't
we?
   I looked you up too. Why aren't you on
Facebook?

Best Wishes
Winter Tour Lover

I am feeling more and more uncomfortable about
all of this. Three times this person has been on my tour
and I am still none the wiser who they are. I don't want
to tell Mum. She has not been the same person since
Dad died and then there was all that fuss with Tim. I
don't want to worry her. The mention of Facebook has
freaked me out.

Thursday Nov 27

Dear Sarah,
   I really feel I could give your tour by now.
Korovin's paintings have a 'thin, flat, fluent touch'.
I think I could make that sound convincing. You
didn't mention his son yesterday. Was that because
there was someone in a wheelchair with us? Did you
see, she nearly ran over the poor gallery attendant's
foot?
   You've only ever said Korovin's son, Alexei,
was disabled and Korovin needed money for his
treatment in Paris. You've not mentioned Alexei had
to have both feet amputated, after a childhood
accident. I haven't been able to find out exactly
what sort of accident it was, mind you. To have your
only child not quite perfect, must be a burden –
particularly a century ago.

54

By the way, your mum seems a nice lady – even if she doesn't like Jehovah's Witnesses on her doorstep. She's a keen gardener too, by the looks of it – even at this time of the year.

If you were in California still, you would be celebrating Thanksgiving. Do you remember your first four Thanksgivings?

Best Wishes
Winter Tour Lover

I can't take this anymore. I'm being stalked. What was he – or she? – doing spying on my mother? I've copied the letters and I'm going to the police station with them. I tried phoning them, but got nowhere. Mum must not find out.

Thursday Dec 4

Dear Sarah,

You're not so perfect after all, are you? When you were telling us about Korovin's designs for the Mariinsky Theatre yesterday, you said Tchaikovsky's 'Sadko', but it is Rimsky-Korsakov's opera.

If you're not feeling well any time, I can always stand in for you.

Oh, and you don't have to look around the whole group, before you start speaking – none of us is going to escape, before you've finished. Each week, we all look so different, don't we?

Best Wishes
Winter Tour Lover

At the police station I eventually talked to a woman wearing electric blue specs. Why do the police not look like the police anymore? Looking at her computer, rather than me, she said, abruptly, "You had online abuse – a couple of years back?"

"Yes. It was some idiot boyfriend I'd dumped, who couldn't let go."

"But at the time, you said it couldn't be anyone you knew."

"Well, I was wrong and if you're thinking it could be him again – it can't. He now lives in Australia and I would know him if he turned up every week – even if he was in disguise."

She picked up my letters and skimmed through them.

"These letters don't actually threaten you, so as unpleasant as you may think them," – she stressed the *you* – "I don't feel we can do anything for the moment."

"I wasn't expecting you to turn up at the museum and arrest anyone."

She almost laughed. "Well, we'll keep the letters and if anything actually threatening occurs, just let us know."

She obviously thinks I'm paranoid, because of what happened two years ago. Fine. I'll sort this out myself.

"If you need to contact me, please do not call me at home – only at work. I don't want my mother to know about this."

Today, there are twelve of them. I think I can discount Japanese tourists, but apart from them, it could be anyone.

I hurtled through the talk like an express train, while most of my brain was concentrating on each person, in turn. It could be all of them, or none of them and after five times, surely something should click when I look at someone. The talk over, I ushered everyone out of the gallery – it was almost closing time, after all. This is not how I should be behaving towards the public, but I am too rattled by now, to think straight. Thank goodness, this is the last *Winter Tour.* Dare I hope that Winter Tour Lover will tire of their sick joke and give up?

After a much needed cup of tea I headed back upstairs to the Education Office. John was there.

"Sarah. There's been a report of some damage to one of the Korovin *Winter Scenes.* Weren't you down there earlier? Would you mind going by and checking it out?"

What on earth was happening now?

"Are you okay, Sarah, you look a bit pale. I'll send someone else down there, if you want…'"

"No, I'm fine. I'll go."

So now they had moved on to actually physically damaging university property. Fantastic! The police would be out like a shot for that and then, perhaps they might take me seriously.

When I got down to the gallery the attendant was still there and inspecting, *Winter Landscape with Two Wooden Huts* very closely.

"What's the damage?"

"Look for yourself," she said standing aside.

I peered hard at the painting. "I can't see anything wrong with it."

"That's because there is nothing wrong with it, Miss Snowflake."

Still staring at the tiny figure in the snow I tried not to move, or look like I was panicking. All I had to do was reach the fire alarm by the gallery entrance and all hell would break loose.

She laughed. "Don't worry. I'm not some knife-wielding madwoman. I just wanted to meet you. No one ever notices gallery attendants, do they? Did you seriously think I was disguising myself every week, just for your benefit? You flatter yourself."

She was right. The same person had been sitting there all those weeks and I had never even glanced in her direction. Attendants come and go. I slowly turned to face her. She was about my age, with black bobbed hair; wire-framed specs; sounded American and looked... well, normal.

"I know this sounds weird," she continued, adjusting her specs, "but the café downstairs is still open, so could we go have tea – and just talk? I've a lot to tell you."

The café would at least have more people. "That sounds a good idea," I said feebly. "I think you have a lot of explaining to do."

She headed for the gallery entrance and the stairs. As I followed behind, like her pet puppy, I was secretly thanking the architect who put the glass-sided stairs right in the middle of the museum, where everyone using them could be seen. When we reached the café she picked a table right in the centre. Only a few were still occupied, but that was enough to make me feel I could handle this. I was trying not to look her in the eye, as we sat down opposite each other, but it was difficult.

I took a deep breath. "Why, all this...?"

"Let's cut to the chase, shall we? I'm your sister."

"What?"

"You heard. Your parents never told you, did they? Mine didn't either, but it's the truth."

The waitress arriving to take our order gave me time to look more closely at my sister, the stalker. I wanted to say there was no resemblance. I wanted to say she was mad. But I couldn't. Her mouth, her chin...

"We'll have two teas," she said to the waitress, "I love British tea." Then without pausing for breath she leaned across to me. "I'm Abigail. That's *Father rejoiced,* in Hebrew, did you know that? Sarah is *Princess.*" She giggled. "Little Princess Snowflake."

Why was this stupid girl, laughing at me? I was no longer scared – just angry. "If you're my sister, why have you been tormenting me with this cat-and-mouse game? Why didn't you just turn up – you found our house – and explain, or talk to me after the tour? That's normal behaviour isn't it?"

"Aah, well, that's because I sometimes see the world differently from other people – I'm bi-polar, with a few other related bits and pieces of disorders. But let's come to that in a moment. I can see there's still a part of you, that doesn't believe me."

She was right there, but I let her continue.

"I was born in California too. My parents Daniel and Elizabeth had IVF. They created embryos and one of the embryos implanted, created me. A year later, they decided they did not want any more children – I was all they needed – so they donated the other embryo to your parents, Alexander and Emma. You were now Alexander and Emma's legal child – you're called snowflake babies, now – out of the freezer and into your new mother."

My brain processed what she said, but I couldn't form the words needed to reply.

"Daniel and Elizabeth died in a car accident, ten years ago, when I was twelve. We had lived in Minnesota for five years, by then. I ended up with a relative and then in care, and then back with a relative, as I was getting into all sorts of trouble. When I was eighteen, my bi-polar disorder was finally diagnosed and I wanted my aunt to hand over all my parents' papers and estate to me. Now I knew the reason for my strange behaviour, I was sure I could finally sort out my life.

It was then, I found all the copies of the paperwork surrounding the embryo donation and at the same time, something else finally made sense to me. When I was about nine, I'd been in trouble at school yet again and my parents had sent me to my room, when we'd got home. I'd snuck back down the stairs and creeping past the kitchen door, I couldn't help but hear my parents arguing.

Mum was crying and Dad was shouting, "What's the other one, like? Like Abby? I keep thinking what would it have been like, the other way round." Then Mum was shouting, "You can't say that. Don't even think it."

"The other one was you. They were wondering, whether you would have given them less heartbreak – when I was only nine years old. Just imagine, how that made me feel when I was eighteen and just diagnosed."

Neither of us said anything for a moment. I could not cope with this. "But how…?"

"The papers contained all the donation details and I knew that one day, I would find you – *must* find you. I wanted to find out who, and what, you were. It wasn't difficult finding your father on the internet – he was a prominent person in medical circles, wasn't he? – the great British surgeon who worked in California, before returning to Oxford. So Oxford was where I was going to come one day when I had cleaned up my act – and find my sister. So, here I am."

I just sat there, staring at her. When I didn't reply, she babbled on.

"But I suppose having found you, I should tell you that my parents – *our* parents – were artists, bohemians, or whatever you want to call them. They drank a lot – something you do in Minnesota, in the winter – and that's how they died. They wanted to be loving parents in their way, but they did not know how to deal with me and their lives were just one disaster after another, anyway." She shrugged. "That's all you need to know about them, really. Once I got here, I just wanted to find you. But I did not want to find you perfect – to find the child my parents really wanted. I wanted to find you, just as screwed up as I am. But then my mind took over and got mixed up, as only it can do. I didn't mean to frighten you, or your mother, or ruin your life. I just get taken over sometimes and then I regret it. Now I've met you, I don't care, if you're perfect – or not. It really doesn't matter any more. So now you know and I'm sorry. I'm sorry. That's what you want me to say and I mean it. Sorry."

For a moment she looked as though she was going to cry, but she just hitched up her specs – the same way I do – adding, "The good news is that I leave next week and you can go back to your life, without me interfering in it."

The tea arrived and she busied herself pouring for us both, before pushing one of the cups across the table, towards me. Concentrating on the milk jug, I managed to finally form a whole sentence. "I can't take all this in, but I do know that my parents – Alexander and Emma – will always be my parents, who brought me up and loved me and there's nothing that you, or anyone else, can do about it."

"Of course. But just tell me you feel better knowing what happened, while your Mum is still alive and able to talk about it, with you. Finding out from a load of old papers, is not the same as hearing it from a person, believe me."

Then she laughed. "What did you think of my English English – not bad was it? I must write more letters."

She stood up and threw some coins and a piece of paper down on the table. "The least I can do, is pay for the tea and that's my address in Oxford and back in Minnesota." I think Korovin would have liked Minnesota – it snows a lot. Come check it out yourself, sometime."

Then she had gone.

I sat there in the empty café, until the waitress came to clear the table and whisper apologetically, "We're closed now."

I rushed straight home and dragged Mum out of the kitchen. "Sit down. Listen. Don't speak."

Then I told her all about Abby, the Winter Tour Lover.

"I think I knew something like this would happen one day," she said, when I had finished. "I wanted to tell you when you were eighteen, but your Dad did not, and when he died, I still kept silent in his memory, which perhaps I should not have done."

"But now I do know, it's not going to make any real difference to us, is it?"

"No, of course not," she said hugging me. "Abby could have actually done us a favour. We have no secrets between us now. Do you think we should invite her round, before she goes back to the States? No hard feelings?"

"No. I don't think I could take that yet, but perhaps one day we could get together, on neutral territory. It will take me a long time to process all of this. The thought of not being an only child has to grow on you, although I quite like the idea of being a snowflake."

"I think it's a wonderful description. But you know, Sarah, the most important thing about a snowflake, is that each one is unique. However deep the snow, each flake is a separate creation and when you look, closely – each one is perfect."

She stood up. "But please, please, promise me, that your next tour theme will be *Summer*."

About the Author

Margaret Bulleyment began writing fiction after a long career in comparative education.

This encompassed an international school in Stockholm, an American High School on a NATO base and teaching Music, English and Expressive Arts, with diversions to the former Czechoslovakia and a children's opera workshop in Canada.

She has had short stories published in anthologies, including *Café Lit,* and on story websites; her children's play *Caribbean Calypso* was runner-up in 'Trinity College of Music and Drama's 2011 International Playwriting Competition' and she has twice had short plays performed professionally, as a finalist in the *Ovation Theatre Awards.*

The Snowman

David Hook

The man sat on the bank and watched the stygian-like river sluggishly flow by, heavy with a mix of snow and grey ash, more viscous paste than water. Every so often a tree or branch would drift past struggling to reach out of the swirling mire, skeletal and beseeching. Above him the oppressive clouds roiled, tormented by the ceaseless gale and heavy with the promise of yet more niveous corruption.

A shiver ran through his hunger ravaged frame and he pulled the tattered tarpaulin tighter about him. He watched as soot-dirtied snow settled on his gnarled and filth encrusted hands; hands too cold to melt even the smallest of flakes.

Somewhere off to his left a splintering crack followed by a dull thud signalled the fall of yet another cadaverous pine. The demise of the tree heralded stronger winds and that meant a blizzard was headed his way. He would have to find shelter. He reattached his snow shoes and rising on trembling legs he gathered his few belongings and began to climb his way back up the river bank, his breath a pluming mist freezing his matted beard. His eyes watered and his cheeks burned as his tears froze.

Reaching the top of the bank he scanned the bleak, lifeless landscape. What was once a mixture of verdant woodland and flourishing farmland was now shrouded in grey frozen slush. Trees, once tall and proud now stood decaying and rotting, stripped of leaves and bark and bleached white by hardened frost. A gust of bitterly cold wind bit into his face as he continued to scan the surrounding area. Another gust momentarily cleared the murky fog and driving snow and, at some distance to his right, he spotted the outline of a building before it was once again enveloped in the miasma.

Drawing on his dwindling energy reserves and fighting against the grime-laden snow which increasingly blew horizontally at the behest of the howling wind he began trudging in the direction of the building.

The building turned out to be an old pumping station which at one time had fed water from the river to the farms nearby. The only door to the structure stood ajar and the man cautiously peered through the gap into the frosted, tenebrous interior. Within nothing stirred. He gripped the edge of the door and began to pull and tug, wincing at the protesting squeal of the rust fused hinges. As soon as the gap was wide enough, he crossed the threshold and instantly felt a wave of relief at being out of the driving wind and pelting snow-ash.

In the centre of the room stood the old pump, long ago stripped of parts. To his left were stacked a number of wooden pallets and much of the floor was strewn with old, faded newspapers and rags. He couldn't believe his luck. Drawing a shuddering breath he rasped a single word, 'Fire'.

To his right stood a utility desk thick with dust and grime upon which lay an assortment of items. A tin cup, enamel chipped and discoloured with age. An oil lamp pockmarked with corrosion, its wick a blackened nub. To the left of the lamp a cardboard box, patchy with mould and listing heavily with damp. Within the box a mix of cogs, gears, nuts and bolts all ocherous with rust. On the wall above the table hung a calendar showing 'December 2021' and depicting an old tractor partially covered with fresh, pure white snow.

The man shuffled to the table and reached for the lamp and suddenly froze. He immediately recognised a pungent stench, urine! Something or someone had urinated in the corner next to the table and from the strength of the odour more than once and more alarmingly, it had been recent. He spun around and scanned the room again. There was nowhere a person could hide and he could see no evidence of a large animal having been present. Tensed and alert to possible danger he went back to the door and furtively checked the snow outside for footprints other than his own, there were none. He sighed with relief and pulled the stubborn door closed.

He began gathering up scraps of paper and small lengths of pallet wood and built a small fire which he then lit with his fire steel. The smoke would sting his eyes but the warmth would more than compensate. His mind wandered back to the piss soaked corner. It had been weeks since he had come across another human being and the chances of stumbling across someone in a place as remote as this was unlikely; even so he pulled a small axe from his rucksack and placed it next to him.

He sat close to the fire and waited for its warmth to thaw him and the room. Occasionally he would glance at the corner and then the door, then return his gaze to the fire. His mind began to wander as he relaxed, back to before all this, to a time when it didn't snow in July, a time when he worked at the University teaching history and strolled in parks under clear blue skies. Back to when he had a wife, a son and a daughter. Sunday lunches and dozing in front of the fire with a full stomach and the sound of children's laughter.

Leaning against the pump he reached beneath the many layers of clothing to a breast pocket and pulled from it a small plastic bag within which lay a faded dog-eared photograph. His wife smiled coyly at the camera. His son, front tooth missing, was laughing whilst his youngest, his daughter, clutched a teddy and stared wide eyed desperately trying not to blink. His hand began to tremble and his eyes blurred with tears. He returned the photo to the plastic bag and placed it on top of his rucksack.

It had been three years since the ash began to fall. Shortly after, as crops failed, the food riots began. The governments, along with law and order, disintegrated and neighbour turned upon neighbour. As the skies became clogged with ash the global temperatures had at first risen leading to cloying humidity and raging storms and floods. Then, as the ash clouds became ever denser, the Earth was thrown into a state of perpetual twilight. The rays of the sun were reflected away from the cloaked planet and it rapidly chilled and then froze.

Crops continued to fail, withering and dying in the frigid, sterile earth. Livestock that hadn't already starved froze where they stood. At first the scavenging mammals, birds and insects thrived before they too began to starve, turning on each other or falling prey to the deadliest scavenger of all – man.

Family pets were consumed. He himself had fed his wife and children their beloved labrador Thorn and even the Koi carp from their garden pond had ended up on the dinner table, 'Fish and chips' he had announced with a wan smile.

The last main staple of the city dwellers were the resilient and resourceful rats, they in turn feeding upon the dead. And when the rats were no more, man turned on man.

The lone and the frail were the first to die, murdered and consumed by roving gangs of ravening cannibalistic thugs. Savage and brutal they slaughtered without mercy anyone weaker than themselves.

How had he, a history professor, survived for so long?

The damp wood in the fire hissed and popped and broke his reverie and he again glanced at the urine soaked corner. He was still unnerved by it, enough in fact, that he grabbed a small length of rope from his rucksack and shuffled over to the door where he proceeded to tie the door closed. It wouldn't hold for long but it would certainly give him some warning and time to act should anyone try to gain entry.

He returned to his place by the fire and threw on a couple of extra pallet scraps and watched as the smoke drifted towards the small broken window next to the door. It was far from a perfect chimney but it would do.

He retrieved the tattered photograph and laid himself out in front of the fire, resting his head against the rucksack.

As his wife smiled at him his stomach gave out a loud, rumbling growl followed by several less plangent gurgles. "Dinner time," he whispered to her as he reached into his coat pocket and produced four walnuts and six dried apricots, the remains of a dozen or so of each that he had found scattered on the floor of a health food shop several days ago. Taking three of each and returning the remainder to his pocket he began to eat.

He washed the morsels down with two small sips of water from his flask which he had filled from the toilet cistern of a petrol station the day before. His supplies were dwindling and he made the risky decision to check out the farm buildings that must be nearby in the morning, assuming of course that the blizzard had abated by then.

He took one last look at the photo and closed his eyes. Exhausted, he soon fell asleep.

The same dream, always the same.

The young woman stood ankle deep in the snow-ash in an alley between ransacked industrial units. Her hair greasy and dishevelled. Her floral summer dress filthy and torn, left breast exposed, gouged and bleeding. Her once incredibly beautiful features now pallid and gaunt. Rivulets of blood trickling down the insides of her slender, pale legs, congealing around her bare ankles and feet. Her eyes, sunken, glazed, absent of any and all emotion.

Tensing he surveys his surroundings for signs of a trap. Unable to discern any he begins to inch forward. The woman continues to stare blankly ahead, unaware of him, the biting cold or her lacerations.

He recognises her for what she has become, a Muselmann, she's nothing but a Muselmann. He inches closer, still she does not move or show any signs of awareness. He reaches into his rucksack and grips the handle of…

He awoke with a gasp and sat bolt upright releasing several shuddering sobs. Wiping tears from his eyes he shivered and looked to the fire, it had dwindled to a small mound of glowing embers. Moments later, after he had rebuilt the fire, he lent back against the pump and stared into the flames.

Muselmann, the word kept tugging at his thoughts. He remembered explaining its meaning and origin to his history students, a German term widely used among concentration camp inmates to refer to prisoners who were near death due to exhaustion, starvation, or hopelessness. The young woman had been the very epitome of the word. Once a beautiful, vibrant young woman, full of hope and life but then just a shell, a violated, tortured, listless husk.

Cuffing away snot from his nose he attempted to shake the image of the woman from his mind. He needed a distraction and reached into his rucksack withdrawing a battered crossword book and a pencil stub.

Outside the blizzard had begun to subside, the howling wind dropping to a whisper. He would be able to check out the farm buildings in the morning after all.

The man tried to engross himself with a crossword but his eyes felt heavy and gritty and he found himself reading the same line several times. With a yawn he placed the book back into his rucksack and picked up the photograph of his family. He stared at his wife and smiled, "So beautiful" he whispered. He kissed each of their faces and again laid himself out in front of the fire. Maybe this time he would sleep without dreaming of the Muselmann woman?

He lay watching the shadows cast by the fire cavort and dance on the ceiling. He closed his eyes but instantly they were open again. A sound, movement! His heart thumped as he slowly sat upright. He listened intently, there it was again, barely audible but definitely a sound, a movement, something small and alive coming from the direction of the stacked pallets.

Without turning he reached for his axe and gripping the handle tightly he began edging towards the stack. With his heart jackhammering in his chest he raised the axe and peered into the gap between the pallets and the wall.

Still crouching, axe poised to strike, he froze. It took a moment for it to register. Sandwiched behind the pallets, one broken wing outstretched, sat a white dove cowering with fright.

Coming to his senses he slowly laid the axe on the ground and wiping his filthy hands on his jacket he reached for the terrified creature. The bird panicked and began flapping its one good wing in a vain attempt at flight but he managed to cup his hands around it and carefully lifted it out of its hiding place.

The terrified bird desperately pecked at the man's hands as he made his way back to his spot by the fire. The man sat and began gently stroking the bird's chest, trying to calm it, to reassure it. Resigned to its perceived fate, the dove stopped pecking at the man's hands and simply sat shivering.

The man was in awe of the dove, it was so clean and white he couldn't stop smiling to himself. If it had been larger, more robust he would have hugged it to his chest. He felt a lump in his throat and tears welling in his eyes. If something so fragile, so beautiful could survive in this bleak, grey, frigid wasteland then surely he could too.

How had he survived so long? He of all people, with no training or experience in such matters. He shook the thought away and returned his gaze to the dove, cooing and stroking it.

The man woke with a start. How long had he been asleep? It couldn't have been more than a few minutes, thirty at most. The Muselmann dream yet again, she plagued his sleep like a gaunt and desiccated Incubus, tormenting him relentlessly, night after night. Never moving nor speaking, her visage alone enough to wrench him from slumber.

Damp with chilled sweat and shivering with both the cold and residual fear he leant forward and placed several additional scraps of wood onto the fire. He noticed that the photo had fallen onto the floor and he retrieved it. Wiping dust from the plastic housing he stared again at his wife, his son and his beautiful, insouciant daughter.

The fire crackled with renewed vigour as he stared into the flames. Every so often a drip of fat would fall into the flames and sizzle briefly.

How had he carried on like this? How had he survived with the ever present danger of ambush, with the gnawing hunger, the biting cold and nightly terrors? All this suffering and horror conspiring against him, to crush his will, sap his strength and lay waste to his resolve.

A large drip of fat spat and burnt his knuckle.

He raised his eyes to the dove slowly roasting over the flames and lowered them again to the pure white feathers, plucked and strewn about him. He closed his eyes and saw the Muselmann, her once beautiful face clear in his mind's eye, only this time her countenance held a slight, knowing smile.

He shook her off and in doing so caught sight of the photograph. Of course he knew how he had survived, for he would never be allowed to forget, the Muselmann would see to that.

Forlorn sobbing turned into a single, soul piercing scream as he pressed his palms to his eyes.

How had he survived?

He ate the beautiful things.

About the author

In 2014 David left a stressful job after many years and found that once his mind had decluttered he was able to focus on long-forgotten hobbies. Writing has become one of those hobbies. David has had several pieces published on CafeLit and was one of the chosen authors in The Best of CafeLit 3.

Worlds Apart

The Viking

"I can find no trace of a nerve," said Mr Easton as he completed an examination of the molar cavity. "I'm sure I removed it all last Tuesday, but root canal work can take some time to settle down, Mr Fellaway. There is still Novocain in your system after the initial operation plus the amount you've had today, so to avoid endangering your health, I'd like you to take this packet of analgesic tablets home and if the pain persists take two every four hours as instructed on the packet."

Murmuring his thanks through deadened lips, Teddy Fellaway took the packet and made his way home that evening to inform his partner, Ruth, of the outcome.

"What you need is a strong cup of tea," was the first thing she said.

"Christ, he's pumped me so full of that bloody drug I'm seeing double of everything," Teddy mumbled miserably.

"I've got to say you look like something out of an old Hammer film but I can't put a name to it; Quasimodo, maybe," giggled Ruth as she put the kettle on. She turned suddenly serious and said, "It could be that Novocain has a deeper affect upon you than it does other people."

"I'm with you there," grumbled Teddy as he sipped the hot brew, favouring the sound side of his mouth. Settling for a light evening meal, they tumbled into bed much earlier than usual with Teddy preparing himself for another bad night. He must have got some sleep because it was ten past twelve when he was awoken by unmerciful stabs of pain. Swallowing two of the analgesic tablets, he drifted off into an unsettled sleep.

It was three in the morning when he surfaced again, this time so muddled, he fell out of bed, and so as to not awaken Ruth, he dragged on his dressing gown seeking the sanctuary of his lounge armchair. Losing patience with rubbish TV programmes he turned the set off; slipping the remote control into a pocket of his dressing gown. To keep the room steady, he shut one eye, focusing the other on the ornate plaster rose in the ceiling, forcing himself to think how fortunate they had been to find a well-cared for nineteen thirties house such as this in Warminster. Far better than the thrown up semi they'd just sold in Shepton Mallet.

Wearing of this, and guessing Ruth would probably look in on him after she'd discovered his absence, he slid down in his armchair absolutely exhausted.

All at once, the door opened to reveal, not Ruth but a man, his exact double, entering the room. Teddy's drugged up mind immediately rejected the image, only to demand a second look. He sat up in his armchair and went cold: this guy was the spitting image of him down to the last facial blemish. But there the similarity ended. The stranger's sandy hair was plastered down with some glutinous dressing giving it a copper-like sheen, and his choice of apparel was absolutely dire. The guy's shirt collar was puffed up in the manner of an Elizabethan ruff, but worse still, he wore a leather jerkin, pantaloons and sandals with toe appendages akin to the fingers of gloves.

Evidently not noticing Teddy, the stranger scanned the room and frowning, consulted a globular wristwatch before striding to the door.

Ablaze with indignation, Teddy hollered, "Hey, who

the hell are you? Get out while you can walk or I'll kill you." Receiving no reply he grabbed the remote control from his dressing gown pocket and threw it as hard as he could at the apparition's head that was rapidly disappearing behind the closing door. The remote control shattered against the doorframe, littering the carpet.

Teddy retched, and stumbling to the bathroom was physically sick, after which he sat on the bathroom chair trying to gather his thoughts. A chill ran through him; *was he going mad*?

Horrified by the possibility, he staggered back to the lounge realising he was too scared to go back in. "*Show some guts, you chicken hearted bastard,*" he raged; "*this is your house, not his.*"

Barging into the room, he raised his fists ready to take on the weirdo whatever the cost; but there was no sign of the stranger. Still enraged he searched the entire house but came up with nothing.

Irritably he dragged himself back into the lounge and flopped into the long-suffering armchair.

He must have dozed off again for the next thing he knew, another personal image had entered the room, but this time accompanied by a perfect replica of Ruth, her raven hair piled up in a cone. They unfolded an enormous chessboard on the floor setting it up for a game using chess pieces eight inches high. By means of electronic hand-sets they began the game. At the touch of a button, a pawn from the activated black army marched on stumpy legs to challenge white pawn that, acknowledging defeat, toddled off the board and deactivated. In this manner the game proceeded.

Eyes bulging, Teddy got to his feet trying to let loose a scream but was only able to make the incoherent noises peculiar to nightmares.

It was then the real Ruth rushed into the room with her hands clasped to her horrified face. She sobbed, "Teddy why are you making that horrible noise; you're frightening me."

Teddy turned, and still incapable of speech pointed to the couple waging war on their incredible invention.

Ruth's gaze followed his outstretched arm in bewilderment. She gently pulled his arm down staring urgently into his face. She pleaded, "What is it you can see, Teddy? Tell me?"

Finding his voice, he croaked, "Can't you see what's going on in front of you, Ruth? Can't you see two people resembling us playing silly buggers with an electrical chessboard on the floor?"

Clearly Recognising the symptoms of his stress, Ruth put a finger to his lips and took him unresistingly back to bed telling him he'd had a nightmare…

By seven thirty the next morning, it all seemed absurd as Teddy tipped cereals into their breakfast bowls while Ruth poured coffee. Teddy moved to her side, placing his head against hers like a child seeking comfort.

Ruth kissed his good cheek and pointing to the packet of pain-killers on the kitchen table she said, "I've never known you to have a nightmare like that in all the time we've been together." Passing a cup of coffee to him, she opened the packet and said, "Take two of these as the man said, and eat your breakfast; you silly boy."

With a wan smile he gulped the bitter medication with a mouthful of coffee, and pushing his breakfast away, he said, "No, it wasn't a nightmare, Ruth, because the TV remote control is lying in pieces on the carpet." He explained the earlier incident to her, his every word turning Ruth's face a shade paler.

"I've got to get to the bottom of this, or I'll go nuts, it's going to be risky but I know what I have to do…"

He took the tablets at four hourly intervals throughout the day and more at midnight before settling back in his armchair to await results. His head swam as lack of sleep and the cumulative drugs took effect. Moments later the door opened to disclose a different but equally incredible scene…

Teddy and Ruth lookalikes dressed in cane ribbed combat dress, and wielding quarterstaffs, strode to the centre of the room; that to them was evidently a sports room. Completing bows of respect, the man made the first move by lunging at Ruth's head, but parrying the blow, she floored him with a scything strike to his ankles. The next round saw him immobilise her with a swift thrust to her solar-plexus.

After another two rounds with honours even, both parties bowed to one another and left the room.

The whole thing had been acted out in silence as before, but Teddy was intrigued to notice this time both contestants had tanned skin and hair arranged in ancient Oriental warrior style…

His overworked mind shut down rendering him comatose until the morning.

Breakfast was a joy to eat; at last his jaw at last responding to the medication. He discussed with Ruth who would be the most likely person to understand what was going on.

She slyly replied, "Why not try old Harry Beamish? He's into UFOs and things; don't you remember him? We teamed up with him in a pub quiz at the Sword and Buckler a few months ago. He's a retired psychologist with an insatiable appetite for the paranormal; so he reckons."

"Yes, of course, old Harry; I'll give it a go."

Half an hour later Teddy located him in the saloon bar, earning the gratitude of a barmaid trying to get her head around the theory of time-travel.

Harry spun round on his bar-stool at hearing Teddy's voice and boozily greeted, "Hallo Teddy old lad, haven't seen you for ages; name your poison."

Teddy ordered whisky and coming straight to the point said, "What I am about to tell you, Aitch, must be kept under your hat; agreed?"

Sensing a brightening up of his afternoon, the older man instantly nodded. He listened intently until unable to contain himself any longer, he yelled, "You know what has happened, don't you; you've blundered into a few parallel worlds; you lucky old devil."

Teddy looked at him askance.

Harry grinned, "Okay, I'll spell it out for you. Ever heard of different zones of existence?"

"Of course, in science-fiction books I read as a kid."

Harry nodded and said, "Well it's my guess that in your drugged up state your mind dissolved the barriers between our world and several other parallel worlds."

Teddy shook his head in mystification; "I can't believe it," he responded.

Harry took a swig of his drink and wiping his mouth with the back of one hand, said, "What I'm getting at is, the people you've met are you and Ruth living in the present time, but living different lives on planets exactly similar to ours." In the normal run of things, nature keeps order, but you have unintentionally invited them into our world that they are treating as their own; see what I mean now?"

Teddy muttered, "I think so, but why couldn't they see me?"

78

"It's because you initiated the process, and not they. Had they been responsible, you would never have seen them."

Teddy shifted uneasily on his stool, "What will happen next; do you think?"

Harry regarded him thoughtfully, "It's difficult to say, but as you've breached three worlds, is possible others might have been affected causing them to spill like sand through a cosmic sand timer."

Gulping the last of his scotch, Teddy dashed from the pub in high panic. A deep sigh of relief escaped him as he turned the corner of his street. The red brick ivy covered house stood as normal with thermals rippling along the sun-drenched roof. He slowed his charge to a brisk walk as he approached the doorstep. Turning his key in the door-lock, he yelled, "I'm home, Ruth, old Harry's absolutely nuts, he said…"

As the door swung open Teddy could just make out Ruth as she vacuumed the hall carpet oblivious to the cotton-wool denseness of their interweaving equivalents going about their everyday lives in every cubic inch of their home.

About the author

James Sainsbury, a former central heating quality control inspector, began writing in 1990, and after completing a correspondence course had two articles and three short stories published. Upon retirement he noticed his two little fingers were curling into the palms and was told he had Dupuytren's Contracture, a disease brought over by the Vikings, hence his chosen pseudonym – The Viking – all five feet six inches of him. Not your average berserker.

Official secrets

Linda Edmondson

From the garden room, they watched in silence as the slate grey of night became the silver grey of a flat winter morning. They watched in silence as the last seed from the sycamore pirouetted perfectly, until a northerly gust from behind the potting shed funnelled it towards the house and it slid down the glass. It landed on the window frame, in front of the three scented candles that sat dormant, waiting for dusk. He picked up one of the candles. Yes, there would probably be enough wax in it for tonight. With the other hand he rubbed her upper arm, gently. Her cardigan was draped over her shoulders like a dust sheet over a carving chair, and she stooped, sighing, over the windowsill.

"Sit on the bed, love. Sit down for a minute." She turned towards him, and nodded a little.

"Yes. Help me over." He pummelled the pillows, creating a wall of softness at the back of the day bed, and she sank onto the duvet.

Outside, the sky had a milky look about it. Then, the sun passed over the guttering and filled the garden room with shafts of cool morning light.

"God's turned the lamp on again." The words wheezed out, and as she laughed the pillows moved with her. "I hoped it would be a nice day today, and it is."

She took his hand, to stop him from adjusting the blanket. She traced the contoured veins and trailed her fingertips along the silver hairs above his wrist.

"Your fingers are cold." He cupped her hand and blew gently across her nails, which had taken on a purplish tone.

She relaxed into the pillows, exhaling another long, crackled breath. Her eyelids dipped, flickered and closed. For a moment he held his breath with her – his mouth open and slack like hers – but he remained silent as he placed her hand back on top of the blanket. After a moment, she breathed again. His heart jolted. She had not left him. Not yet.

"Can I get you anything?"

"Cuppa would be lovely, please."

She stirred when the china clinked as he placed the tray on the side table. As he apologised for waking her, she shook her head.

He sat on the bed, her thighs providing lumbar support, and looked into the garden. The sun freckled through the trees and the branches danced. Leaves collected in eddies over the frosted borders.

"I don't think it will be long, now." With her words, he blinked and looked into her. Still, he did not speak. "Thank you for looking after me so well."

A tear tracked down his cheek. He did not touch it. He gulped, but still did not speak.

"I need to tell you something… before it gets too tiring. Before it, it begins to happen…"

He drew breath.

"No – let me finish." But instead she paused. The rasping from her chest echoed, long after she finished exhaling. Again, he tried to match her breathing pattern, holding her hand ever so slightly too tightly.

"When it's all done, when you've phoned everyone you need to, I need you to… go into my grey work bag… Before I go on, get a pen and paper." She gestured towards the drawer and he frowned as he left her, to fumble for the materials. "So, you need to go into my grey bag, on the coat rack I think, and in the front pocket there's a little black notebook."

He looked from her towards the bedroom door and began to walk over to the coat rack.

"No, not now." Her voice was crisp, like it had been. "Sit back down here and I'll tell you what to do."

Like the obedient Labrador that he often was, he sat back on the bed. Then he licked the tip of the pencil.

"On the first page there are some phone numbers. I want you to call the third one down. Write it down, the third one. I think it begins 0207 64... I can't be certain of the rest." She paused again. "Anyhow, when you get through, make sure you are speaking to Amanda... and tell her that you need to get a message to Elodie."

"Elodie?" He looked up.

"E-L-O-D-I-E." Another long sigh sucked her deeper into the pillows. "And then, just tell her that Snowflake has... melted."

"Snowflake?"

"It's my code – my nickname. Tell her what's happened... give her details of the arrangements. They will want to come."

He finished writing and put down the pen. "And, are you going to tell me what this is all about?"

"Help me sit up. And pass my tea. Is it cool enough?"

By the time they were ready to continue the conversation, the sun had poured into the garden room, casting bronze shadows from the wooden window frame across the bed.

At her suggestion, he lay cradling her.

"So... Elodie? Snowflake? What on earth's this all about?" He tried to say it softly; she should not see his frown-lines.

She breathed rapidly and he felt her rigidity. For another moment, he held his own breath, but rather than the deep final sigh that he expected, she began to speak again.

"You know, I often wondered how I would tell you, when... if... the time came." He exhaled, relieved not to be making eye contact as she breathed rapidly a few more times.

"Sometimes, well, I wasn't giving extra language classes to my students. Sometimes I wasn't going on exchange trips to Normandy. Sometimes... I was just a good old fashioned spy." As he gasped, he felt her body soften and as he looked down he saw her cheeks grow; he was not sure if it was a smile, or a grimace. "There, I've said it. Forty-four years we've been married, and I did my bit every year, for Her Majesty."

He blinked repeatedly and tried to focus on the fine cracks on the ceiling; tried to count to ten rather than say anything too spontaneous. Today, despite her revelation, was not a day for a counter attack. He felt her relax a little more, or perhaps it was just that he had tensed up; he was not certain. In silence, they watched the leaves whirl, as the bare branches of the wisteria clacked a drum march on the window.

But then she held his arm, quite firmly.

"You might have a few questions... about it all. If you do, today might be a good day to ask... considering—"

"Could you say that again, please?"

"Must I repeat myself? It's hard to say once—"

"Just tell me, again, what this is all about?"

She sighed. The silence that followed startle him once more.

"I was recruited in our final year of college. I think my knowledge of Polish, from Babcha, tickled them. By the time they realised it was mostly folk tales and family recipes... I was already well into the programme." Her breathing quickened again, like she had just run a race.

"I'm, I'm flabbergasted. I had no idea."

"I was very good at what I did."

"Clearly." He looked at her profile. How the cancer had sharpened her features. How thread veins meandered down her cheekbones like rivulets down a rainy sand dune. Her breathing vibrated her cardigan. He did not know how to respond.

"Most of it was mundane. Easy to do while you were at work, or while my class was busy with something. A lot of translation... lots of banal messages. The key was to look for patterns, for oddities. I think that's why they called me... Snowflake. I could spot things – symmetry, you know. And I had to learn about funny things, too... especially early on."

"Like what?"

"Like whether the first Spanish strawberries really were on the supermarket shelves, on a particular day. It was all very Le Carré, I suppose... I found it quite funny, you know..."

Another pause. No, I don't know, he thought, but didn't say.

"... Talking about good days for washing the bedding, and all that... Clearly our Allies were also recruiting a lot of housewives at the time."

The sun caught a silver frame hanging near the door, illuminating the photograph of their children, playing on the beach in Newgale all those years ago. They both looked at it, for a few moments. He thought how her voice had sparked at this morning's revelation, and now rattled like an old engine. It had been a long time since she had had the energy for such a conversation.

"Don't you have any questions?"

He got his handkerchief out of his trouser pocket, wrapped a corner of it around his index finger, walked across the room, and wiped the top of the photograph of Andrew and Amelia. You could see the sand on their round, white bellies. She had taken the photograph, he remembered, on the Leica. He'd wondered at the time how they had managed to afford a camera like that. He couldn't remember her explanation.

"Questions?" he looked at the skin stretched across her cheekbones, and how the sun cast shadows in her eye-sockets. She was not looking at him. He doubted that she wanted the sort of questions that one needed to ask following such a revelation. And as she regained some momentum, she rattled on, as he expected she would.

"Later on, I did a few *site visits*, so to speak. They soon lost their appeal, though. There was so much to think about, tasks to get out of the way…"

He twisted the handkerchief in his hand. "What do you mean, tasks to get out of the way? Do you mean? Did you, did you ever, you know—"

"Kill anyone? Is that what you are trying to say? No, no I didn't. Well, not directly, anyway." She twirled her wedding ring, which hung loosely beneath her knuckle. "One never had an inkling about what happened as a result of one's actions… it was all very need-to-know."

Her eyelids fluttered, as did her breath. "Who'd have thought a conversation could be so exhausting, eh?"

Exhausting would not have been his choice of word. Astonishing, possibly, or incredulous, yes. He screwed his handkerchief into a tight ball and put it back in his pocket. Then he counted to ten again, in his head.

"Love, you need to sleep for a bit. We can talk later."

"I hope so."

He tried to think as he washed the cups and prepared egg sandwiches and a jug of cordial. He frowned as he hacked slices off a pineapple, which she had requested but he knew she would not eat. He took her to the toilet, and while she had a moment's privacy he swapped the pillows around and thumped them hard and turned the duvet and tried to think, again.

Then he re-lit the three rose-scented candles on the windowsill, to mask the sweet uncertain smell that had lingered in the room over recent days.

He tried to think as he watched the flames stumble when the breeze crept through crevices in the window frame. He went back into the hallway and turned up the thermostat before they both shuffled back to the garden room, arms and hands linked. They settled back onto the duvet and he propped the tray of dainty food and barley water on its stand, on the bed. She took the smallest quarter of a sandwich.

He tried to think, but his thoughts made no sense, so he did not share them.

"This Elodie you mentioned, does she know a lot about what you did?"

She licked at a corner of the sandwich and paused.

"I suppose so. I worked with her long enough. Right up until all this business took hold."

"Right." He put down his drink. "In that case we'll talk no more about it. Not today, not tomorrow."

"Don't be like that."

"I'm not being like anything. I'll talk to her when I know what I want to ask." He straightened his back and looked deep into her eyes. "You've surprised me, very much. I'm stunned, actually. And a bit confused. No, a lot confused. A lot. I had no idea. None, whatsoever. I wish you'd been able to tell me, before." He did not want to look at her. This was not how today should be, with his voice raised and his fists clenched.

Her eyes were fogged. You could see the pain etched into her crow's feet. Each breath fought against the heavy weight in her chest.

"Have… you… not… heard of the…Official… Secrets… Act?"

"Yes, but I'm your husband." Speaking more softly, he looked at the trees and grasses waving in the dying light outside, and wiggled his fingers. "I never thought there would be surprises like this, especially not now." He stooped and scratched his head.

Now it was her turn for the tear to build.

"Peter, don't be like this… Not today." As she reached out to touch his hair, he turned towards her and shook his head, very slightly.

"If I'd known before I'd, I'd have had time to be proud of you, not cross and confused." She mirrored his closed-lipped smile and took his hand.

"And that's exactly why I wouldn't tell you about any of it. It worked because I could be normal… because you wouldn't think anything special of me… Because then you wouldn't give anything… away. Sorry, I didn't want it to be like this… either."

"But I can ask Elodie… afterwards?"

"Yes, you can try. But then she might have to terminate you—"

He stopped the joke. "Is there anything else that you need to tell me?"

She put down the sandwich. He could barely make out where she had nibbled it.

"Only one thing, really, and you know that already."

"Just say it, again." He held her hand again, as she whispered.

"You were… are… the love of my life. I love you… have always loved you. Dearly."

He gulped, nodded, and the tide of tears ebbed again.

"How am I going to manage without you?"

"You will, my love… You will… I'm just going on another trip."

"Another jaunt to Normandy?"

"No, somewhere more exotic… Ascension island, perhaps…"

"Gosh, you did travel a bit."

"I did." She drifted again. "The sea was so warm…" They were silent. Perhaps he could think, now. Or perhaps not.

The final pools of sunlight were a deep yellow. Watery tones of ochre and crimson flooded across the end of the bed. Outside, the breeze had tempered, and those remaining leaves that chose to be sky-bound in the last minutes of daylight floated towards the freezing earth in a cascade of gilded confetti.

He watched her late breaths again, and timed the growing pauses between them. Quietly he took the tray back to the kitchen. He did not wash the cups. For a long moment he stood with his hands splayed on the worktop, looking at her finger-marks on the sandwich. Then he made two short phone calls to Andrew and Amelia before returning to sit with her, until the only light in the garden room came from the flickering candles.

A harsh exhalation startled her. He stroked her cold arm and switched on the bedside light.

"Shush – it's OK. I'm here. The children will be here soon, too." She nodded, and within minutes returned to her rattled rhythm of sleep. He could not match her pattern of breathing.

"Constance, what a dark horse you have been, my love."

With his muttering, she half opened an eye. "I told you… never… to… call… me… Constance."

"Shall I call you Snowflake instead, then?" He shook his head with the bewilderment of it all, but there was the faintest of smiles on both their lips. Until her smile flattened.

"There is something else… actually."

He closed his eyes and rocked backwards. "Oh, what now?"

"No, Peter, this is good…Really it is… In my grey bag, there's a building… society… book—" she gasped as she tried to squeeze the words out. He knelt before her and willed her to breathe again, which she did."

"I'm OK, Peter… OK… And so will you be, when you see the money that's accrued… from my little escapades. You look a little… shocked."

"Not for the first time today, you've astounded me."

"Well, when you've paid off the children's mortgages… take me back… to Ascension. Find a beach… scatter me among the green turtles. I'd like that."

"May I kiss you?"

"Since when have you needed permission, Peter?"

"Since I discovered I really don't know that much about you! No, no, I'm still not cross. Confused, yes. But not cross. It's not how I thought today would go."

Their lips met, parting only when the doorbell rang. She smiled as he promised to be straight back, and again she closed her eyes as he hugged the children and their partners, hung their coats over the grey bag, and hugged them all again.

Their murmurings stopped as they entered the garden room.

Her lips were slightly open and the corners of her mouth rose in a delicate bow. The only sound came from the guttering candles on the windowsill.

About the author
Linda Edmondson lives in Littlehampton, West Sussex, with her family of assorted and much loved two- and four-legged creatures. Linda is a member of New Writing South and enjoys crafting short stories as a happy distraction from finishing her first novel (aimed at teenagers), or from doing her 'proper job' (writing and editing educational materials for health care professionals).

Between the Flakes

Roger A Price

I awoke around 9 a.m. Not that I'd slept much; my legs had ached on and off all night. I just couldn't seem to keep them still. When I did doze, all I dreamt about was getting my next fix of heroin. I was glad it was morning; nearly time to go and 'score' from my dealer, then maybe the pain in my legs would stop. But it wasn't just my legs; I seemed to ache all over it was just worse there. The cold didn't help.

I slowly orientated myself out of bed; I felt slightly heady and had to wait a minute for the 'mist' to clear. Then, the coughing started. I rushed to the sink where I was violently sick. That over, I steadied myself against the wall whilst I recovered, glancing around the hovel my squatter's room had become. Spartan. Anything of value had long been taken and sold for drugs. There was no heating, no hot water, nothing. How the heck had I let my life reduce to this, barely an existence? A single bed – with sheets I hadn't cleaned in weeks – was the only furniture. I hadn't washed the covers because I couldn't be bothered as it didn't seem important. Cardboard was taped to the window as makeshift curtains, and the cold dew held them to the panes. It wasn't very effective. Maybe after I'd scored later I would sneak down to the household tip and see if I could find some old cloth. Mind you, that would mean playing 'hide and seek' with the council workers: 'smack heads' weren't welcome there, 'smack heads' aren't welcome anywhere. And especially at this time of year.

I splashed some water on my face and cleaned my teeth with my finger, before putting my shoes on. They were still damp from yesterday's trudging through the snow. I was already dressed; I never got undressed, as there seemed little point. I then realized I was starting to shake and shiver; and not just because it was cold. I was starting to 'rattle', I had to get some gear soon, it was only going to get worse, a lot worse.

I picked the purse up off the floor and took out a ten pound note; it was full of notes, tens and twenties, over £300 in fact. I hadn't checked the rest of the purse, never did, I was only interested in cash. But, as I took the note out, a wave of guilt hit me; what kind of man had I become? One who could steal from an old lady.

Her bag had gone before she'd known it, and I'd been off before she could have done anything. That had been last night when she'd left the cinema around midnight. She'd probably been working there and on her way home. I hadn't hurt her or anything like that. In fact I'd made sure so; I was quite adept now at sneaking up from behind, cutting the strap on a shoulder bag and taking it before the owner knew anything. I never hurt anyone, though I knew plenty of 'smack heads' who did. Even so, she must have had one hell of a shock, but I was desperate. I'm always desperate. All that ever matters is getting enough money for my next bag of heroin. Mind you, I'd hit the jackpot this time, over £300, I couldn't believe my luck. I was due a bit of good fortune. That amount of money would keep me 'sorted' for a few days at least. And, I could buy some proper food instead of the usual rubbish I ate, which mostly came out of skips at the back of the supermarket.

Anyway, time to get going. The dealer would be open for business from 9.30 a.m. That's what he'd said last night after I nicked the old dear's bag. It was around midnight when I rang him. "Too late," he'd said, he'd sold his last bag. I'd have to wait until the morning. That's why I'm starting to suffer withdrawal symptoms; I'd missed my late night fix.

I'd hid the purse in my room in the squat; other addicts were always coming in and searching it, looking for things to nick. Thieving swine would have probably overdosed if they found all this. But it was too risky to take it out on the street with me; I was always being turned over out there. This neighbourhood had really gone down the pits; it used to be such a nice area a few years ago. I'd lived around here all my life, though I didn't recognize the place now; but I don't suppose the place would recognize me either.

Back to the matter in hand; no, I would only take a tenner, just enough for one bag of heroin that would see me right until the afternoon.

I walked out into the daylight and squinted as my eyesight adjusted. It would be worse once I'd scored; my pupils would let in too much light. It would feel like you do when you've been to the pictures during the day and come into the daylight. I remembered going to the Saturday matinees as a kid. That brief memory soiled, as the thought of the cinema brought a fresh feeling of guilt at last night's activities. I shook it off. The enlarged pupils would be a small price to pay.

As I walked down the road a snowflake landed on my nose, I shook it off; that was all I needed. In doing so I caught my reflection in a shop window, it made me stop and stare; I knew it would be bad. I was in a bad way, but the sight still gave me a shock. I hadn't seen myself for a few days; I tended to avoid mirrors, nothing good to see. Though I hadn't expected this; I looked a real mess. I needed to rein things in a bit; my habit was getting worse. Squinting once more at my reflection, I wondered how I had come to this. From being a twenty year old undergraduate with a bright future ahead, to this in just over a year. It didn't matter where you came from, or what kind of upbringing you had had; heroin ignored social classes. It crossed all divides, and united all within its misery.

I shook my head and ignored my self-distain, I had to get going. The quickest way to where the dealer lived would take me past the cinema; and therefore past the corner where I'd robbed the old lady last night. I didn't want to go past that spot. It would have been all right in a day or two, but not nine hours later. My self-loathing reminded me of its presence. I paused, but the only other way was across the park, and that would take twice as long. Ten minutes delay, no way; that was too much. I kept going the same way, kept my stare down at the pavement.

I turned a corner. *The* corner. The one from where I had sneaked up on the old dear. She never saw me; I always approach from behind, quick in and out. All she saw was the back of me. It wouldn't have been too bad for her after all, I reckoned.

Then, I rounded the corner and almost walked straight into a copper. That was all I needed. I mean I had no worries; I hadn't scored yet, so I was clean. He wouldn't find anything if he stopped and searched me, I could just do without any delays. So, I kept my head down and walked past him, whilst muttering, "Sorry mate didn't see you."

"Just a minute Son," came the reply.

I hate it when they call you *Son*. I wasn't his son. My own father had died years ago, so the only person's son I was now, was my mother's, and I hadn't seen her in months. It only made her cry when she saw me, and as soon as she stopped lending me money to 'sort myself out', I stopped visiting. Her definition of 'sorting myself out' meant getting off the gear, getting cleaned up and eating properly. My understanding was very different; it went straight on more drugs. And when she realized this, she'd stopped doling out the dosh. So, I'd stopped visiting. Another wave of self-pitying remorse touched, if only briefly. I was having a hard day today. It would be better once I'd scored, though I had to deal with this copper first. "Yes Officer, how can I help you?" I said as normally as I could, conscious now of my appearance.

"We are looking for witnesses to an incident which happened here last night. An elderly lady was attacked," the Officer said.

"Sorry, I can't help you. I wasn't around here last night," I lied. "Anyway, what exactly happened?" I thought that was pretty smart of me, remembering to show normal interest, even seeming concerned, like the good citizen I no longer was.

"An elderly lady was robbed," he answered.

Keeping up the interest angle, I asked, "Is she alright?" Knowing, that she was.

"No, I'm afraid not, she had such a fright it brought on a heart attack, and at this time of year as well. Happy Christmas from a scumbag."

His answer hit me with the speed of my first fix; but without the pleasure. "She can't have." I stuttered, my swagger and arrogance replaced with horror as his words sank in.

"Afraid so Son, there are some real slime-balls around here nowadays. It used to be such a nice estate, good hard working people who looked out for each other." The Officer said.

Frantically, I asked, "She's not, er you know…"

"Dead?" the Officer said, finishing off my question, "No, she's not dead. But it was touch and go through the night."

By now, I had forgotten about all my woes, all my aches and pains. I just felt disgusted in myself. I felt unclean, on the inside as well as the outside.

The Officer went on, "We are trying to trace her next of kin. Apparently, she has a son who lives around here. Though, she's not seen him in a while, you might know him? He's called John Smith."

At this point, my world shattered, completely. I thought I'd misheard at first. I asked the copper for the name again. I received the same reply. I paused, and then spoke, "I'm John Smith," I said. My self-abhorrence and feelings of guilt now utterly real, and not fleeting. I knew this was it. Enough was enough; this had to stop, and stop now. "Lock me up Officer," I said to the startled policeman, "lock me up and I'll tell you everything. I did it, but I swear I didn't know it was my mother. Not that that should make a difference; if she wasn't my mother she could have been someone else's. But I'm going to need the Police Surgeon; I'm going to need some help, it's time to sort myself out."

Twelve months later, I left prison a changed man. It hadn't been easy; here drugs were on offer inside, but I'd resisted. I'd taken all the help I'd been offered. One day at a time, each easier than the last, and I'd done it. I'd been clean for several months, and if I can resist it on the inside, then I can avoid on the out. But, before I put my life back in order, there was one thing I knew I had to do first; especially at this time of year.

I'd spent a year practicing what would happen next; as I came to a halt by the T junction entrance road outside the prison. Left was to my old squat, which had no doubt been taken over, though I wondered if the hidden purse and its contents were still there; probably not.

Right would put me on a completely different course; one I knew I had to take. A soft flake of snow landed on my nose as the weather started to turn. This time I didn't shake it off. I felt it melt and I listened. I had already decided on what I had to do, but this little flake from a flurry that had stopped as soon as it had started gave me that extra little push. I turned right and set off to make my peace with an elderly lady who worked at the cinema; and to wish her happy Christmas from an ex-scumbag.

About the author

Roger A. Price is a writer of crime fiction. After thirty years in the police he retired as a detective inspector and draws from those experiences to inform his writing. He has published two five-star rated novels with more on the way. Further details are available via his website: www.rogerapriceauthor.com

Brown Christmas

Paul Bradley

It's Christmas day. I'm twenty-two and sat here in my bedsit by the sea. It's the kind of place local councillors are always bleating about in the local press. Houses of multiple occupation that attract ex-convicts, the unemployed and drug users. Apparently, ruthless buy to let landlords encourage some of them here by advertising dole by the sea in regional papers across the country. I'm an unemployed drug user. Heroin. Wrapped up in my little 'opiate cocoon' as the drug books say. I've got enough gear to last a week plus some to sell and I've stocked up with instant food too. Biscuits, crisps, tins of ravioli, instant mash, flapjacks. Not that I eat much anyway. If I need anything I can steal it. Nothing to worry about until New Year. I can just use, listen to music and take it easy like the bedsit zombie I am.

There's no one to bother me. Even the benefit office will keep off my back for a while about all those missed appointments and failure to attend interviews. My parents live across the country and they don't talk to me. Last year I broke into their nice semi to steal some money and jewellery but got caught by Dad who was quietly wielding a golf club over my head whilst I rifled through his and Mum's wardrobe. Dad rang the cops and we waited silently for them to arrive. I knew Dad better than to start sobbing and pleading. That would make me even more detestable in his eyes. He's ex-military. Charges were dropped eventually; my mum probably had something to do with that. No need to worry about seeing the family. They can keep their Quality Street, Marks and Spencer's deep filled mince pies and crappy James Bond repeats. The queen can stick her speech where the sun doesn't shine. None of it matters to me. Just gear and the rush that comes with a spiked vein. That's all.

Or so I thought. Last night, I actually started to let a few emotions back in. Wandering back home through town rekindled old feelings from the past at this time of year. I actually took notice of the decorations: neon snowmen, Santa and holly in shop windows or strung along electric wires high above the streets, church bells ringing loud, the big Christmas tree and its lights in the town square, groups of town folk earnestly singing carols around it. Everyone wrapped up in hats, gloves and scarves. One part of me liked all that and another thought it twee. This town by the sea is much bigger than the village I grew up in with my sister and parents but it reminded me of that place last night.

Another thing happened on the way back to mine. I noticed the latest Rupert Bear annual prominently displayed in the local bookstore window. The eternally young bear looked as eager and happy as ever with his plain red jumper, yellow chequered scarf and matching trousers. I stood there for ten icy minutes gawping at that book. Forced myself to remember, to look back and recall a time when reading all those magical stories made Christmas that extra bit special. Every year I'd get two Rupert Bear annuals. One would be the latest and the other would be an old one tracked down by Dad. I thought about my parents and how they used to tell everyone about my love for Rupert. How they would catch me under the covers late on Christmas night with a torch reading about his adventures. I used to imagine I was really with Rupert and his pals in Nutwood. Rupert's deep sea adventure when he met King Neptune was my favourite. What a world to escape to.

Shop windows don't just display coveted items to tempt passers by. They reflect the image of the window shopper too. I could see my image clearly last night, the windows offering a bright perspective due to the street lights and overhead illuminations. The purple tracksuit I always wear is a shocker. No style. No class. Black trainers nicked from Oxfam. My body is thin and pointy and cheekbones define my face. Then there are my teeth. Rotting away, falling out, deep yellow and brown, pink gums receding. It's easy to imagine how I'd look as a corpse in a chapel of rest. To think I was captain of the school rugby team and top in English Lit. I started to feel rough and, aching for a hit, headed off home.

Home is a first floor bedsit in the middle of the promenade. Walking up the threadbare burgundy stair carpet last night I knew that Rupert, family, Christmases past and my physical appearance would soon be wiped clean out of mind and replaced by sweet nothingness. I opened the door, walked in and switched on a light. The place stank of old food, cold stale air and me. No decorations except a couple of cards from customers on the floor and, by the sink, a saxophone playing Santa that I nicked from a Poundstretcher store. It lay on its back with the sax pointing to the ceiling.

Instead of settling in straight away to a night of oblivion I stood near the door and looked around. One room. At one end a small kitchen area that looks like it should be part of a 1970's lifestyle museum. Light green painted cupboards with plastic handles, stained formica surfaces, dirty yellow ripped linoleum flooring and a rotting sash window with a soiled view of the fire escape. A large blue flip top bin overflows with empty beer cans and black streaked foil. The sink full of caked dishes.

I scrutinized the rest of this room I call home. On

one side a torn mustard coloured two-seater sofa with foam sticking out of its arms and two legs missing. A cracked glass coffee table heavily ringed with mug stains takes up the centre and a portable TV with a mini aerial occupies a corner on top of a spindly brown table with wonky screw off legs. A few feet from the TV is an old electric fire with a ripped plastic false coal flame effect with wooden shelves down the side which carry only dust. The walls themselves are a filthy cream nicotine colour and the carpet, which leads up to the linoleum, is grimy lime green. Things don't change much here, they just deteriorate. Walls get yellower and legs fall off the sofa.

Near the window overlooking the promenade I sleep on a small single mattress on the floor. It's damp over there and the wallpaper is bubbly. The old mattress is stained and smelly and sleeps like a hammock it's so knackered. My dark blue duvet cover, flung across sideways, has caught a damp pattern off the wall. The pillow has no case and no substance consisting of a mixture of blood, beer, fag burns and vomit stains. Close by is a small round metal waste paper bin. It's got a print of wild cattle like beasts going around it in the style of a cave painting. I pee in it at night because I can't be bothered to go out to the landing to the bathroom I share with the bloke upstairs. With the duvet around my shoulders I kneel, balance and then pee into the bin, moving the trickle and stream around, making a musical splashing sound that changes tone with the depth of urine. I then have a hit before going back to sleep, slopping out when I wake up. Then there are the curtains. Faded dark green with a lighter spiral pattern and always, always closed.

I opened those old curtains last night. Then, for the first time, I heaved the sash window upward and leaned out a bit. My stomach ached and I was sweating despite the cold. I could smell the salty sea. Street lights lit up the prom and I could see the dark rising of the waves beyond the metal sea barrier. They rose up closer and closer, the tops silver with the light, continually poised before crashing against the sea wall sending showers of spray and stones across the road. Over to the left stands a kiosk that sells ice cream, snacks and novelty gifts in better weather. I could just make out the daily special etched on a board inside a side window. Tea or coffee with a buttered scone and jam for £2.50. To the right in the near distance stands a short decaying Victorian pier that looks as though it would go out to sea if the sea would have it.

Without warning, still half leaning out and looking at the waves, I felt tears on my face. I don't know why but the views provoked within me a cloying nostalgia for my old infant school and the crayon pictures of rainbows on the classroom walls. All the kids would sing "Red and yellow and pink and green, orange and purple and blue. I can sing a rainbow, sing a rainbow, you can sing one too." Light snow danced and pirouetted gently down from the heavens and a gathering of flakes itched my nose. Definitely time for a hit.

I walked over to my stash. Foil, lighters, syringes, straws, spoons, lemon juice, a bag of brown gear, skunk weed, king size Rizzlas, filters, tobacco and a packet of Camel cigarettes all kept on a large metal TV dinner tray near my mattress. I picked it up carefully, sat on the old sofa and decided to chase the dragon. I placed a small amount of heroin inside a folded strip of tin foil and heated it up from underneath with the flame from a yellow lighter. The heroin turned black and wriggled around whilst I chased the fumes with a shortened straw. Within minutes I started to feel a warm glow in my stomach and then the kindness spread all over. Nice and dreamy and just content.

I smoked a cigarette. Usually, I smoke roll ups but I decided to smoke a Camel or two to celebrate Christmas this year. A treat. They were on special offer at bargain booze. I lit up and sent a cloud of smoke into the centre of my room. I watched it linger, almost blue, before it dispersed up down and sideways. No thoughts to bother me now. I just existed, smoking a cigarette. No deep and meaningful reflections, just inhale, exhale and watch. Doors slammed upstairs and I could just make out some raised voices but there was no need to pay any attention. I simply sat back with my eyes half closed and let time do as it will.

When I came round I had a great idea. In a cupboard there were a few old batteries so I fetched them along with the saxophone playing Santa. Before long I had old Santa on the coffee table churning out the tunes; 'Old King Wenceslas', 'Rudolph the Red-Nosed Reindeer', 'Silent Night'. His hips were swaying jerkily to the sound and his head nodded up and down with the sax at the same time. It was some show. Next, I turned on my CD player, plugged in the headphones and put some heavy dance music on. I just sat there watching Santa with the volume up high and I swear the old man from Lapland kept a perfect rhythm for every single track.

It's funny as hell watching Father Christmas straining away with so much enthusiasm to a fast dance tune and each time he stopped I picked him up and pressed the button at the back of his red cloak to start him off again. The cigarette smoke added a kind of Christmas jazzy atmosphere and I felt good about this world and my place in it. But those old batteries didn't last too long. I noticed that Santa started slowing down more and more until he ended up just swaying his hips every now and then before stopping in mid flow. I took off my headphones and pressed Santa's button a few times. He managed a quick shimmy and the final stalled notes to 'Silent Night'. Time for a real hit. I cleaned up my abscessed left arm, boiled the kettle, let it cool, adding a tiny amount of water to the junk on a teaspoon along with a little lemon juice to help it all dissolve, before warming it all up with a flickering flame underneath. Taking a new syringe out of its package I stirred the mix, placed a cigarette filter on the spoon and then sucked the junk up into the syringe before injecting a declining vein found by using my phone charger wire as a tourniquet.

Almost straight away I was overwhelmed by a rush. It felt like a world-wide climax that could only be resolved by death. I must have read that somewhere. But it was that good. My eyes closed and I leaned back into the sofa, staying in this dream state for some unknown time until suddenly brought back. On the coffee table Santa had burst into a swinging rendition of 'We wish you a Merry Christmas,' dancing and playing like a dervish. It was nearly midnight. As far as I know Santa hadn't played that tune before. As soon as he finished the final note he stopped playing. It seemed like some sort of sign.

I've been thinking about last night. The decorations, the carol singing, Rupert, family, this bedsit, nursery school, the musical Santa. It's hard to make sense of it all but I can't go on like this. I'm going to get clean after the New Year. Start again. Contact the family. Get that Rupert annual. Detox. Methadone or Subutex. Rehab. Maybe even some work. Right now though I need a hit. Happy Christmas.

About the author

The author lives and works in North Wales. He enjoys a number of hobbies including hill walking, swimming, reading and writing. As regards writing, the author tends to enjoy social realism, with writers such as Raymond Carver and Richard Yates being a couple of favourites. A number of short stories have been published in the small presses, and a children's story has recently been published in an anthology called *Strange Tales V* by Tartarus Press. The author has a son called Oliver who is currently studying at Cardiff University. All his written work is dedicated to him.

Snow Woman

Jo Fino

It had been a long deep sleep, the kind which takes time to have an effect. Martha stretched out her sated limbs, and inhaled. The air was different. Overnight something had changed. The small child rose within her and she struggled from the jungle of sheets, padded across the worn carpet and tugged at the heavy curtains.

Snow: it lay below in thick piles, fitted over grass and pathways. On the hillside above crawling jelly-coloured tots trailed sledges in bright sprawling lines. She dragged on an old oversized sweater, thick socks and faded denims, ran down the back stairs, thrust her feet into old boots and wrenched open the kitchen door. Before her lay the virgin garden. Martha stepped out slowly, sighing at the first creak of submission. Then, with a wild shriek she launched herself onto the white mattress landing face first in the icy snow, her nose scorched by the cold. She raised her face and laughed rolling over and over, arms spread eagled, supplicant to the snow god.

"What on earth do you think you're doing? Get up. You look ridiculous." It was Mother's rasping voice.

"Just look at her, Mama. You can't leave her alone for five minutes. She's an embarrassment. Don't you think it's about time we did something about it?" Her spoilt sister, Rosie, Mother's favourite.

"What do you expect Rosie? She's not like the rest of us is she?" The modulated tones of her older brother, Jack.

Martha closed her eyes, shaking her head from side to side, snow sticking to her cheeks and ears. The voices. Again. This couldn't be. They were all gone now.

"Look at her. What *is* she doing? You'll have to keep her out of the way when Sam's family come for dinner. Please Mama."

"She's just attention seeking. Ignore her sweetheart." Mother's voice always softening for Rosie.

"Why don't you send her to visit Auntie Cynthia? She never seems to have any trouble with Martha."

Well done Jack. She loved Auntie Cynthia. They were muttering amongst themselves in the kitchen now. Martha scooped soft snow into her ears and closed her eyes. She stayed very still, willing the melting snow to numb her lobes.

When Martha finally sat up and looked around she couldn't hear anything except the slow silence of the snow. Good. They were gone. She would write about them in her diary later. It was her secret. And Auntie Cynthia's. She would sit quietly in the corner carrying out small jobs she was deemed capable of doing and listening. They didn't know she had a good memory. She was very precise, noting down everything they said and everything they did. In the margins she doodled little pictures of them. Auntie Cynthia said she had a gift. She missed Auntie Cynthia.

A movement from the white laden bushes in the border distracted her and she caught a flash of red. She cooed softly. "Hungry little robin?" He flitted over to the birdbath and tapped the solid surface. "Thirsty too?" The robin flew to the glistening holly tree and settled to watch while Martha chose a stone from the crusted rockery and launched it into the centre of the ice. It broke with a satisfying crack and she used the stone to mash the ice up.

"Put that stone down at once. You're going to break the basin you idiot." Mother; back again.

Martha dropped the stone in the centre of the birdbath, a sickening crack signifying the inevitable, iced water splashing her boots.

"See what you've done. Come inside at once."

Rosie sighed. "Daddy's going to be so upset with you Martha. He loves watching the little birds splash about in that birdbath. Hope you're proud of yourself."

Martha stared at her boots, a tear trembling at the edge of her icy lashes. The robin warbled again. "Okay little man, I'll see if I can find you some breadcrumbs." She looked back at the garden; watery sunlight was filtering through the heavy snow clouds. She hoped it wasn't the beginning of a thaw. She had waited so long for the snow to come again.

Every winter when the snow came she had watched through her window, the glass misting over as the children streamed down the hill. She had ached to join them but Mother said it was too dangerous and not fair on Jack and Rosie to have to look after her. One winter Daddy spent days in his workshop while Mother muttered over bubbling pans in the kitchen casting black looks in his direction when he came in to eat. When the snow finally began to fall Daddy unveiled his masterpiece: a sledge with high sides and a seat in the middle they could strap her into. Martha clapped her hands, scrambling onto the sledge as Rosie and Jack stared on resentfully. Mother turned on her heel, retreating to the kitchen without a word. That night the first fall of snow melted away, taking with it Martha's dream, and they enjoyed the mildest winter for years. By the following winter Daddy was stuck in his chair by the window and the sledge was inhabited by a colony of spiders in the darkest corner of his workshop. Rosie and Jack eventually moved on from the hope of the annual pilgrimage to the hillside but Martha had continued to watch, waiting for the snow to come again. Now it was her turn.

Martha left the robin and went back to the house. Everything was in its rightful place in the kitchen; no dishes in the sink, no lingering seductive scent of caffeine. Mother always had a hot pot of coffee ready at breakfast; not that Martha was allowed to have any. Mother said it would make her jittery. Warm milk for her. She wrinkled her nose in disgust at the memory of the smell and how her stomach would heave as she gulped it down A puddle was gathering on the kitchen floor around her sodden boots and Martha bent down and pulled them off quickly, throwing them into the corner where they landed in a clattering heap. She slid across the stone floor in her thick damp socks and filled the kettle halfway before carefully measuring the coffee grounds into the jug, a shiver running through her as she breathed in the rich aroma. Four good spoonfuls. She had noted it in her diary.

"Mr Robin! I forgot!" Martha grabbed some bread from the bin, tearing it into tiny pieces onto an old tin plate. It was her plate. Mother never could bear the thought of an odd number in her china dinner service.

Ten minutes later, the breadcrumbs set outside the door for the robin, Martha settled in the sacred front parlour where she had rarely been admitted, a steaming mug of coffee in her hand. She savoured the smell, delaying the first gulp of heaven before sinking into the chair, sipping slowly.

"Mother, I can't have her at the wedding. Everything has to be perfect. You know how important it is to me." The voices were behind her now, in the hallway. "Rosie, I have to say I think you're being unfair." Was Jack really sticking up for her? "Weddings are about families. Martha should be there. Surely Sam's family will understand that."

"Understand? He's standing for election next year. For God's sake Jack, you should know what that means. How would it look if it came out that his wife's related to a mental case?"

"She's your sister. How can you talk about her like this? Mother please speak to her."

Martha shrugged herself deeper into the armchair.

"It's Rosie's future we need to think of Jack. If she loses Sam she may not have such good fortune again."

"Good fortune? If they can't accept that Rosie has a sister who is a little bit different then what kind of people are they? What kind of people are we Mother? Time moves on and so should we."

Martha knew Jack studied a lot of books, heard Mother talking on the telephone, telling her friends how well he was doing at 'the office'. She wasn't quite sure what that meant but it seemed to have changed Jack. Sometimes he even asked Martha about her day and what she had been doing. She remembered now.

"And what about Dad? Is he excluded too? We can't have him dribbling all over the wedding cake can we?"

"Jack!"

Martha shrank further down in the chair, afraid they would smell the illicit coffee.

"They know Daddy's ill, Jack. It's not his fault. He can manage to come to the church, and the reception for a while. Rosie, I'll ring Auntie Cynthia, ask her to bring Martha to church to see the wedding and then back home. I'm sure she won't mind. Now that's the end of it. No more arguing!"

She heard Jack snort, the front door slamming shortly after.

Martha had never heard Jack speak like that to Mother before. She was looking forward to her diary tonight. Except they were all gone now weren't they? Martha sighed and rubbed her eyes, trying to remember as Mother and Rosie's chatter about flowers, hymns and veils faded away into nothing again.

Martha sat up straight. Time to find her sledge. She took her cup to the kitchen, retrieved the damp boots and crossed the back hall to turn the heavy key in the side door. Daddy's workshop was at the side of the house down a small pathway fringed with mature fruit trees. Martha slid down the iced path losing her balance at the last moment and ended up on her bottom, her feet smashing against the aged wooden door. It splintered under the impact. She held her breath. No one came.

There had been too many wasted winters since Martha had visited the workshop. She remembered though that the sledge was stored at the back, guarded from her by the layers of their lives. She clambered through years of memories, stopping to leaf through photo albums made damp and dusty, opening mouldy leather cases labelled with journeys, cradling discarded jam jars that once held her wild flowers. Here was her favourite chair, broken and never fixed, piles of Jack's books, their words too long unread, a rusting bicycle of Rosie's that Martha was never allowed to ride.

She emerged with her prize as the light was starting to fade, the snow hardening in the late afternoon air. The sledge was green and musty, the red and blue paint almost all peeled away. She dragged it up the path and into the house to dry it out. She knew where Mother kept the matches and she knew how to lay and light the huge wood burner. She had watched Mother do it often enough from her little chair in the corner. Once the wood burner was lit she made herself a cheese and ham sandwich, carefully trimming off the crusts. She didn't like crusts. She took it into the cosy back lounge off the kitchen and snuggled up on the settee under a huge tartan rug, nibbling neatly as she leafed through an old magazine of Rosie's. The pages were yellowing now, the fashion photographs faded but it was her favourite; one of the models reminded her of her sister. Martha traced the outline of the yellowing face with her finger, leaving a small grease stain on the cheek from the butter. Rosie wouldn't have liked that.

Martha awoke in the first light of early morning on the settee, stiff and cold. She looked around with bleary eyes. Where was Mother? She would normally be bustling around making toast and brewing fresh coffee for Jack before he went to the office. Hushed tones drifted from the kitchen, not the family though, these were unfamiliar, male. She drew the blanket closer around her.

"Yes, the auntie was the only living relative. Moved here a few years ago, after the fire. This last year after she had the heart attack, Martha nursed her auntie day and night. Very close they were."

The other voice murmured a question Martha couldn't quite make out.

"I hear she's a little eccentric, but not dangerously so…"

Martha pushed off the blanket and walked across the room, hesitating in the doorway. The kitchen was empty except for her sledge, the heat from the wood burner lingering. She brewed more coffee before climbing the stairs to change. Her bedroom window was still open from the day before, the room ice cold and full of distant screams from the hillside: the children were sledging already. Today Martha would finally join them, maybe even help to build a snow man. She took fresh clothes to the kitchen, dressing hurriedly in front of the wood burner.

"What are you doing in there? Aren't you dressed yet? Hurry up!" Mother was outside the door.

"Mother we're going to be late for my dress fitting. Just leave her be. She'll be fine. Come on, the taxi's here." Rosie, whining for attention as usual.

Martha could hear Mother tutting; she didn't like loose ends. "Well, goodbye then dear."

The front door banged and they were gone. Good. Martha gulped down some of the hot coffee and pulled on her boots. The rope on her sledge was stiff from the heat of the wood burner. She grabbed her gloves from the top of the cupboard and a red woolly hat off a peg in the hall way. It was an old one of Rosie's she had kept all this time.

When Martha stepped out, huge flakes of snow swirled in her face, the air thick and heavy, sucking her along. She set off down the lane heading for the bottom field. Through the flurries of snow she could see coloured figures scurrying towards her, larger ones carrying small anoraks with bobbing striped heads.

A voice whipped past her. "Look at that woman Daddy! What's she doing with that big old sledge?"

The snow was so thick now she could no longer see the fence that bounded the field. More people passed her and she turned around to watch them, catching a boot on the edge of her sledge and stumbling. An arm reached out and grabbed her.

"Are you okay? You should get to shelter. I can help you, if you like?"

Martha blinked through the snow flakes. He was a boy, maybe thirteen or so. She could make out red cheeks, blue eyes, a smile. He took the rope from her hand, offering her his other arm to lean on, and gently guided her through the parts of the track that had been well trodden that morning.

"It took us all by surprise," he said, "one minute we were all flying down the slope, the next it's like a blizzard up there."

"I was on my way to join you."

"Really?"

"It was going to be my first time. I've been busy you see, looking after my auntie. She was very ill." Martha stopped talking. Mother always said she babbled. The snow was easing a little and she could make out her house at the end of the lane, the front caked in desiccated grains of white, the roof hanging in iced drapes.

"Is that where you live?" the boy asked, "the big house?"

Martha nodded. "I think I'll be alright from here. Thank you."

She went to take the rope but the boy held on to it and carried on walking beside her. "You live there all on your own don't you? My dad told me. He knew your brother. You're the little sister aren't you?"

Martha didn't say anything.

"My dad was there, at the wedding reception. He nearly got caught in the fire. He told me how quick it spread, the people screaming inside, how his friend, your brother, Jack, went back in, tried to save them, then the ceiling went and they were all trapped. Police never found out how it started did they? You were the lucky one weren't you?"

There. Martha always knew Jack would turn out alright in the end.

They had reached her house and the boy handed her the sledge. Martha smiled at him. "Thank you. You've been a big help. You really have."

He turned to go then swung round. "I can call for you tomorrow. We can go sledging together."

She smiled again. "If you like."

Martha dragged the sledge round to the back garden, her feet sinking deep into the drifted snow. The broken birdbath streamed tiny icicles in a jagged broken grin. Daddy would have loved that. Poor Daddy. She always remembered the way he winked when he lit up his pipe, tapped his nose and said, "Our secret eh Marth? Our secret." Even when he was ill and thought Mother didn't know. And that cheeky twinkle in his watery crinkled eyes, the one he saved for Martha. She saw it that last day in the church, just before she left with Auntie Cynthia.

The garden stretched out in front of her, flowing like a pure white christening robe, the ragged crucifix mould she had made the day before filled in. It was as if she had never been there. Tomorrow she could start all over again.

Martha kicked off her boots, opened the kitchen door and stepped in. It was quiet and cold, the faint aroma of coffee lingering. She picked up the matches and went to light the fire.

About the author

Jo writes short stories, flash fiction and is working on a novel. She is a member of a successful and supportive writing group based in North Wales who have encouraged her to push her boundaries and seek publication. Jo writes for therapy, for fun, to learn and to experiment. She writes because she loves words and the places they take her to as she explores different characters and different lives.

Oh yes it's flaky

Dianne Stadhams

Casting the annual pantomime in Wyeway is a major spectator event in itself. I'm not sure whether it's a penance or a prize but I'd been asked to write a 750 word feature about the opening performance for the local newspaper. I made headlines in the *County Chronicle* last month as the prodigal professor. Five years in Australia and now I'm back on sabbatical. I've a book to complete with a six month deadline.

Devotion's a funny word. It implies exclusivity, focus and passion, mostly directed towards a person or a cause. My sense of devotion is more mundane, an enthusiasm or a mild addiction. What else can I do but read and write? I'm unemployable in any other world. Shy, gawky and hopeless at sport I struck lucky with research.

"Go hide at home," said my publisher, "You'll get the manuscript finished with no distractions."

Done and dusted, easy peasy, so they think. But home is a problematic word. Is home where you are born or where you are accepted? Wyeway or Toowoomba, Gloucestershire or Queensland, Britain or Australia? I am devoted to the idea of a home, always yearning for that faraway place but never quite settled. I return from one home to another with nowhere to hide.

My brief from the *County Chronicle* is to give a fair critique and be honest. If only I dared! Living in the village and being the brother of the script writer 'the truth' poses a conundrum. As I wish to remain attached to my bollocks I will write only what needs to be read. And this year's pantomime has been something else.

A call to read *Snow White and the Seven Dwarves* rallied most able-bodied and feeble-minded residents. 'Break a leg' assumes a whole new meaning when amateur thespians struggle through snow to the village hall by five o'clock. Wet coats, dripping hats and a parade of Wellington boots littered the Wyeway hall vestibule. Inside the motley masses were assembled, gently thawing, scripts in hand. The group was eager to bond and begin.

An evening of literary delight was promised with frozen sausage rolls and as much home brew as you could down in three hours. Frank, the volunteer in charge of lighting and all things technical, prides himself on skolling more pints per hour than Bill in sound effects. It got ugly by the end of the night. The drunks started to argue about the feuds from shows in yester years. Others vomited in the toilets and missed the pedestals despite the large poster above the washbasins.

Your HOME AWAY from HOME!
Take pride - this is your place.
Each and everyone is responsible for
the care of this village hall.

Alcohol was banned one year by the Village Hall Committee (VHC). Consensus transferred the script read-through to our local pub. That meant paying retail prices for beer. Herk, the publican, was delighted and sponsored an annual pantomime award for outstanding achievement. Quite how achievement was to be defined was left loose after heated committee debates. But no one could afford to get drunk at pub prices. This deviation was denounced as 'too boring for words'. It has been back to the village hall ever since, care notices and vomiting thespians notwithstanding. But the post-performance party on opening night is always held at the pub and Herk still offers his award.

I watched as Boris Downey, the Chair of the VHC, greeted everyone at the door with a slobber on the cheek and a limp handshake. His wife, Doris, decked in her Sunday best, but minus her crocheted hat, stood beside him. With a forced smile she indicated the refreshments – entirely unnecessary as the refreshments have been in that place for twenty three years. Ever since a VHC decree was passed unanimously on the grounds that the expense of mop head replacements could be halved through judicious limitation of 'messy areas'.

"Clearly locals are more mindful of where they eat than where they urinate!" I noted to my sister Belinda.

After first drinks or three were downed, the would-bes and the wannabes sat down on the hard-backed metal chairs ready to read the lines. The chairs were placed in a circle, cold to the touch but quick to warm up. Once heated their structural integrity was called into question as tiny squeaks erupt when anybody bits move. I'm told that on the first occasion when the chairs were used, Boris Downey thought one of the VHC had a flatulence issue. Most of the committee chose to ignore the sounds at first. But after a while this became impossible. Doris took charge and tabled an emergency motion to suspend the meeting in the interests of health, safety and social decorum. No farting offender was found, despite Doris's thorough interrogation of all present. The result was a major agenda item at the following meeting. Lots of attempts have been made since that first meeting to rectify the problem. These range from lubricating the chairs with Vaseline, suggested by the womanising rogue who runs the local garage, to knitted joint rings, made by the Women's Institute group that use the hall on the first Tuesday of every month. Nothing has worked. The solution is elusive but Boris has it listed as a recurring item on the VHC agenda under Any Other Business.

There were four chairs placed at the top of the circle. These were reserved for the Writer, the Director, the Stage Manager and the VHC Chair. Boris and Doris donated the maroon, Draylon-covered club chairs to the VHC. The chairs are comfortable enough although in latter years the springs are not what they should be. Incumbents, especially portly ones, get stuck. According to Belinda, the Director had to be heaved out last year. Doris confided to me that the ensuing incident was a ploy by the Leading Lady to cement her bid for the role. She had placed her red-tipped talons into the Director's hands and decorously tugged. This resulted in her toppling from stiletto, knee length, purple, suede boots to land in his lap. Rumour has it that the Director squirmed, the VHC Chair scowled with jealousy and the rest of the cast fixated on the expanse of breast overflowing the décolleté of her dress. The Leading Lady claimed to have fainted.

"Friends, thespians and countrymen, lend me your ears," the VHC Chair welcomed. "In the spirit of the good bard I have come not to bury Caesar but to hand over to Belinda, the writer of this year's script. Her time to rise. My time to praise."

The throng clapped. Belinda looked nervously at the floor. I rolled my eyes and began to make notes. Frank burped. Rosalie, the stage manager, appeared to be assessing the shoes of the assembled as she compulsively folded and unfolded her hands in their fluffy purple mittens. Alice Sweet, who is a dead cert for the role of the Fifth Sheep, was almost beetroot tinged for the whole evening, such is her blushing adoration of Frank, who failed to notice her pining fixation. Doris Downey kept her eyes peeled on the Leading Lady who winked at Boris whenever the opportunity arose.

Belinda is a legend, the local girl made good. Our dad was a farm labourer, barely literate. Sporting ox proportioned pectorals and a dulcet tenor voice he dug ditches most of the day and sang half the night. Star of local music hall he was renowned for his pitch perfect and tear-inducing rendition of *You'll Never Walk Alone*. Belinda and I inherited none of his genes. She was petite and less than impressive as third backing singer with *It's in His Kiss* at the pub's karaoke nights. I never even passed the audition for the Sunday school choir in the nativity play.

What my sister lacked in musicality she compensated with vocabulary. From top of her class in English throughout school she graduated from Oxford University with a first in English Literature and the gold medal for her essay on *Esotericism of the Second Generation of British Romantic Poets 1815 -1837.* The hat trick was landing a job in the media.

"And you are?" smarmed Tom Prince, the celebrity actor, bolstered by fast sex and a diet of drugs.

"Belinda, TV researcher. Gosh, I can't believe you are talking to me."

"A snort or a fuck?" Tom replied.

She blushed. He was amused. They left the party together. Then it all went pear shaped. He got a devoted, uncompetitive live-in, gourmet domestic. Belinda marvelled at her good fortune. She got pregnant and headed home to beyond the hills in order to roost in the family nest. Wyeway was thrilled to herald the homecoming queen and her soap opera king. Who quickly reverted to the pond frog he had always been. I call him the Toad Prince but not to his face. I love my sister and her children despite their spawning. Belinda says she approves of what five years in God's Antipodean backwater have done for me. Such are sibling bonds.

Local sweepstakes reckon that Belinda's husband has bedded every female below thirty five over the last six years. Latterly he seems keen to expand his horizon. On bonfire night he was caught *in flagrante* with the widow Jenkins – not a day under fifty-three. Her departed spouse, a devoted but dull accountant, bequeathed her a large inheritance and a healthy appetite for life. The result was surgically enhanced breasts, a face cranked in permanent smile and the predatory habits of a tom cat. Consensus is that Belinda's husband may be errant but he must be a skilled performer between the sheets.

When the village am-dram committee imploded for the fifth consecutive year after its attempts to collaboratively write a pantomime script, Belinda stepped in and offered to take on the job.

"A local girl with a gold medal for writing is not to be ignored," said Boris.

Her offer was accepted and every female in the village looked forward to reading her work and meeting her husband, although not necessarily in that order.

This year's script, *Snow White,* followed last year's sell-out of *Jack and the Mechanical Beanstalk.* So successful was the engineering that the beanstalk refused to stop growing on the final performance, hit the ceiling, pushed through the trusses and damaged the roof tiles. In turn, this triggered the fire alarms, switched on the sprinkler system and automatically summoned all available fire engines from the neighbouring districts to the scene. It took a week to clear the sodden mess and a protracted meeting to appease the emergency services. But everyone agreed it was the piece de resistance, the finale of a lifetime. I wish I had got to write that feature, warts and wobbles included.

Belinda prefaced the introduction to her script with a direct reminder.

"Snow White needs to make a substantial profit to offset last year's extravaganza. The cost of repairing the hall means that this year's offering must be produced on a much reduced budget."

Boris qualified this when he announced that the VHC had added a caveat: no moving parts to be used in the performance for any reason.

"If this is violated, in any way," chirped Doris, "all performances forever more will be cancelled."

The reading began but all did not go well. Before long, a major dispute erupted over representation of the seven dwarves.

"We don't have any dwarves in the village," said Boris.

"Improvisation will be a challenge," offered Belinda.

Frank suggested using children. Alice clapped approval and added, "It would look cute." Others agreed.

"The performances would be truly inclusive and cement community spirit."

"Bravo, small people are small people whatever the label."

Boris and Doris objected strongly.

"Everyone knows," they chimed, "that children today are undisciplined. We can't have them running amok in the village hall."

"Imagine the cost of the repairs," said Boris.

"We could lose our insurance cover," agreed Doris.

Frank looked askance when he saw the common support for this sentiment. The Director suggested that there might be problems having youngsters around. Something to do with family legislation and police record checks. Boris and Doris were vehement.

"Rubbish. There's nothing funny going on in our neck of the woods!"

Another suggestion was tossed into the debate.

"What about putting folks in wheelchairs? Make 'em look half size."

"Why would you want to that?"

"Where would we get seven wheelchairs?"

"Daft, couldn't get that many wheelchairs on the stage."

"This is not a play about disability rights."

Just when it looked as if the group might agree about the metaphorics of dwarfism on stage, Doris raised the temperature by introducing the thorny topic of which charity would benefit from the proceeds of the performances. No one wanted a donation to go to organisations linked to dwarves. Agreement on this settled the group but not for long. The debate presented lots of options for the target charity – local versus national versus international; children or adults; young people or the elderly, people or animals; buildings or causes. The list was endless.

Finally, Belinda burst into tears.

The hall went silent. Speculation was rife.

"Bet there's something untoward going down at home," murmured Boris to Doris.

"What can you expect with that sexpot husband of hers?" Doris whispered back.

Belinda took a deep breath, put her sodden tissue back in her bag and spoke breathily.

"I would just like to say that we should all remember charity starts at home. If the rest of the meeting is going to be about shouting at each other I would prefer to withdraw my script and leave."

The group did not move. They knew Belinda would not withdraw her script. She has said this every year since she began writing them. The group recognize the signal.

"Enough is enough," said Boris.

"Time to finish," echoed Doris.

The following weeks would be fraught with cast members trying to enlarge and re-write their parts, lobbing the Director for a more prominent role and aligning themselves into factions to ensure their opinion was delivered. It would be to no avail. I know Belinda. She was very serious about withdrawing the rights to her script if a single word was altered without her authorisation. So the ritual went full circle. Rehearsals would start with a whole new round of simmering excitement and cold arguments until opening night. Tales and memories keep the village gossiping for months.

The meeting concluded with Frank staggering from the room to visit the toilets for a relief vomit. He won the drinking competition over Bill with a score of five pints per hour. Alice asked Belinda if she thought Frank had noticed her new shoes as he had spent a good deal of time staring at the floor. Rosalie overheard the question. The look on her face suggested that Alice should pray that nobody noticed what she had on her feet.

"Are you going to check that Frank reads the notice in the toilets?" demanded Doris.

"'Nuff said," muttered Boris.

"It's not you that has to clean up the mess."

124

"It won't be you either luv," replied Boris, "Leave it to the cleaners."

Belinda rang her husband. There was a short flurry of excitement. The women checked their attire and flicked their hair. HE was coming to collect her. His mobile was on but the toad didn't answer. The voice mail message clicked in. Belinda was nonchalant in a save-face kind of way. Others were most disappointed and showed it.

I offered to walk Belinda home. My sister's house was en route to mine. The nudge-nudging began. The Publicity Co-ordinator winked at the Front of House Manager. I knew bets were on for whose bed Belinda's errant husband would be found. The Prompt wagered it would be the widow Jenkins, again. The Leading Lady didn't care because she had had a rendezvous with him last Wednesday. Alice was concerned about how Frank would stagger home and offered to drive him. Frank gagged. Alice blushed. They drifted in separate directions like snowflakes skulking from oak branches before the thaw.

Belinda and I walked in silence for some minutes before she asked, "So who will win the bet?"

"Who told you?"

"Walls and ears – same old, same old," she replied.

"Want to upset the game?"

"Oh no, that wouldn't be cricket Professor."

"Oh yes it is," I replied.

"Oh no, brother dear, let's not start that."

"The old ones are the best," I said.

"Panto," quipped Belinda, "where did it all go wrong?"

"I'll bet on Shirley," I said with resignation. "She knows it's safe to entertain."

Belinda said nothing.

"A woman needs…" I mimicked, "Shirley will say that if it gets awkward."

She is good at justifying infidelity. What with her husband's impotence!

I should know. I'm her husband.

About the author

Dianne Stadhams is an Australian, resident in the UK, with a PhD in communications for development. Described as a charismatic speaker she has a successful track record in global marketing. She has spent many years in some of the world's poorest nations working on poverty alleviation projects. Her website www.stadhams.com gives details about these and her other interests.

Waiting for Susan

Jeanne Davies

At some point deep within the night, snow had fallen serenely, icing the meadows in a soft blanket of white and plunging the country into a blissful muffled silence; a world in suspended animation.

The dogs went wild as we began our walk and soon discovered this cold intangible substance invigorating to roll in. The beech hedge whispered in the breeze as we skirted the lonely cemetery. All the graves lay hidden by the fall, apart from one in the far corner where the floral arrangements had not yet decayed. Draped with snow, the lichen-covered obelisks loomed like bed heads for those sleeping there; a stark reminder of how temporary life is.

A small solitary figure, barely visible under a fountain of half-naked willow branches, stood by the church gate. She was about seven or eight with long fair hair cascading to her shoulders and fanning into a shimmering curtain, which cut across her green coat. One of the dogs charged towards her with hackles raised and broke into a bark. The girl's face, as waxen as a cream camellia, quickly fell into a worried grimace.

"Don't worry, she won't hurt you!" I shouted, quickly whistling Tabitha back to my side.

The child managed a weak smile but her young face appeared sad and care worn. She looked anxiously behind her as though she was waiting for someone.

"Are you OK?" I asked.

"Yes… thank you," she said nervously, like a moth caught out in the daylight.

I felt reluctant to leave her there alone but the dogs were impatient to reach open countryside. We scurried along beside ice laden streams, where clusters of primroses hid shyly along the banks. The dogs knew she was following before I did. I looked back and smiled at her; she drew her satchel nervously over her shoulder and nodded.

Eventually the girl set out along a parallel path leading to Copse Farm. She walked quickly, occasionally breaking into a run but continually looking back to ensure we were in view. I was worried when she stumbled and dropped her satchel into a ditch; but then she waved and continued her journey. As the dogs bounced into the snowy meadow, I saw the child disappearing into a small cluster of farm cottages.

The panoramic views on the horizon caught my breath as we entered open fields bewitched into a wonderland of white. Naked trees held tight to shimmering buds but young catkins danced on the breeze, shaking icy droplets down upon us. A plane zoomed like a rocket high above us, slowly ripping a white scar across the azure sky.

We walked until the greyness of the motorway split through the landscape, and then headed back past the farm where cattle munched on winter's fuel in pens. There were three little cottages in a line near Copse Farm, joined together by their front garden gates. I glanced up at the window of Rose Cottage and saw the little girl waving at me. Her pale features creased into a grin as she held up a ragdoll, all floppy and pink.

The novice sun continued to sparkle in the sky and over the next few days our paths seem to cross as the girl in the green coat would be waiting under the willow, like a snowdrop. The dogs began to ignore her, so each day she'd walk behind us and then I'd watch her go safely along the path to the farm before she'd turn and wave.

One day, I was suddenly aware of her walking beside me.

"What are your dogs called?" she asked.

"Millie and Tabitha… Tabitha is the naughty one! What's your doll's name?"

"Susan," she said, focusing her grey eyes on mine. "I always take her with me wherever I go."

Our paths separated again and she ran off waving.

A few days later, winter made another attempt to hold spring prisoner. Ice cold rain fell in a fine mist, creating a grey gossamer veil over the whole landscape. The fields were flooded, making our usual route muddy and too difficult to take. We pioneered the path like earthworms emerging from the depths. I turned up my collar against the March winds and trudged down the lane to Copse Farm, hoping I'd see the little girl at Rose Cottage. As I walked, head bowed against the wet, something pink caught my eye. I parted some grasses with my boot and there deep in the ditch lay Susan, all covered in mud. I stooped to snatch it before one of the dogs did and headed on towards Rose Cottage, squeezing water from the ragdoll as I went.

I hoped the little girl might be waving down at me from the window, but today the blinds were closed; in fact all the curtains in the cottage were drawn shut. The dogs suddenly became subdued and went to sit either side of the front door, staring at me like sentinels. The sky had darkened suddenly and rain began falling like a curtain; I was grateful to stand under the part-covered porch. I rang the bell several times and then resorted to loud knocking. Eventually a short, stout woman appeared at the side gate holding a red umbrella.

"They've gone away!" she shouted, looking me up and down suspiciously.

"Oh, I see," I said.

"They won't be back for several months; they've gone travelling around the world." She seemed so unfriendly; I could only think she didn't like dogs.

"That's nice; but I think the little girl might be missing this," I said, holding up the bedraggled object. "I found it in a ditch."

Despite the reflection from the red umbrella, the colour drained from the woman's face and her mouth seemed to droop down at the corners. She stared at me hard and speechless. After a while the silence between us deafened me.

"Do you think you could keep it for when they come back?" I asked, gesturing for her to take it. "It might need a bit of a wash," I added.

"Oh no, I can't possibly do that," she muttered, turning her back as if to leave.

"Well, if you'd prefer I can take it home and wash it first?" I suggested.

The woman pivoted around and I noticed pools of tears lying like half moons in the lower rims of her grey eyes.

"No, I don't mean that. I mean I couldn't give it to them; I couldn't possibly distress them by bringing it all back to them... that's why they've gone away, to try and get over it."

I stared blankly at the woman but she seemed to be looking right through me.

"They need to get over the tragedy of it, you see," she said, quickly dismissing her tears with the back of a hand. "It's been several months now and they're still coming to terms with it... they're trying to help each other through it."

We seemed to be holding a conversation in two different languages. The weight of the water dragged my hair down over my forehead in the shape of little worms. The rain on the woman's umbrella made a hollow noise like someone playing a tin drum; and then the beats became a funeral march, melodically playing inside my head. I looked down at the doll and suddenly tears washed with the rain down my face.

"The little girl… she died?" I asked.

The woman nodded like a stoic bulldog on the rear seat of a fast car. "She's buried back in the churchyard over there," she gestured into the distance.

Merry-go-round horses moved sedately around in my head whilst I tried to recall when I'd first seen the girl… it wasn't months ago, but barely a week. The icy rain slid down inside my raincoat like a serpent, slowly creeping along my arms and legs and down to my ankles. Like a deadly poison it turned my whole body numb.

"Leukaemia it was," went on the women, her voice coming from somewhere far in the distance. "Emily was a beautiful little girl, like a delicate flower. Her parents did everything they could… relentlessly took her to every doctor they could find. But it was no good; she was taken from us. It nearly sent her mother crazy; they put her in a mental asylum for a time. It was so tragic… tragic… tragic," the voice echoed.

I stumbled as I felt the ground move beneath my feet.

"Are you alright dear?" the woman asked.

I could feel the heat from her red umbrella and the closeness of her pansy-like face pushed up near mine. "Do you want a glass of water or anything?" she asked.

"Did she miss the doll?" I stuttered, thinking that water was the last thing I needed.

"She cried for it for days when they took her to the

hospice... Susan she called it. They looked everywhere but no one could find it."

I was aware of one of the dogs whining next to my boot. Mechanically I clicked the leads on the dogs... I don't remember if I said goodbye to the woman; it all became a blur. I was still clutching Susan in my hand as I stumbled along the path. How could it be the same girl? If it was, how could I have seen her and walked beside her last week, when she had been dead for months?

I walked alone, holding the modest bunch of flowers. The whine of the metal gate broke the silence of the cemetery. I crept past ancient slabs of concrete where time had completely worn away any engraving... man's final attempt at immortality, failed. The newer stones were pristine and deeply cut with words from loved ones and special vases with holes in, some filled with flowers and others waiting to be remembered. I reverently approached the mound in the far corner where decaying flowers just held on to silhouettes of their previous glory. I had hoped to find a beautiful angel as a headstone, but there was just a simple little wooden cross. I carefully placed the floppy pink doll with the snowdrops there; and I knew that Emily would no longer need to wait for Susan.

About the author
Although being fairly new to fiction writing (having spent most of her life writing words for others), Jeanne Davies continues to gain publishing success for her short stories. Over the past year she has had three flash fiction stories published in anthologies. She lives a country life with her husband and dogs in Sussex.

Snowdrop

Linda Flynn

Fluttering flakes swirled in a dance, celebrating their uniqueness. Silently, stealthily they settled, merging and losing their identity in one solid mass of snow.

At first the heavy door to the wooden chalet seemed wedged shut. Sylvie scraped back some more of the burgeoning, compacted snow from the step and wrenched it open, just a slither, but enough to slide through.

A chill permeated the room as she swept the ash from the grate. All around her she could see signs of the last visit, the red wine circles bled onto the oak coffee table, dishevelled cushions sloping off the sofa and the runched up crimson rug.

She coaxed a flame to shimmer into life and sat back on her haunches as it trembled against the wall. It was not so very long ago; it was another person, a different life time. Only shades from the past danced in the shadowy fireplace.

Sunlight flickered through the slats in the green shutters, enticing her awake. She gave a languorous stretch, then reached out to pull the window open, allowing the dazzling brightness and cold air to burst into the room.

Iridescent, sparkling drops twirled against the pane, gracefully gliding to the ground.

She longed to rush outside, crunching her boots in the crispy snow, indenting pools of her own footprints.

These are my daisy chain days, she sighed, savouring this moment of happiness. Yesterday on the sleigh they felt exhilarated and alive, tumbling, twisting, hurling down the mountain, with their scarves thrown out behind them.

Flocculent snow flew into their hair, flowed onto

their tongues, feathery, fleecy and flimsy as confetti. Their cries whirled into the billowing veil.

With flushed cheeks they had built up the fire, its rosy glow suffusing the room with warmth. Sylvie had placed a flickering cinnamon candle on the coffee table and stood back to watch the burnished walnut basking in the honey glow.

She watched the soporific movement of his breath as he lay cocooned inside the soft, downy duvet. Sylvie snuggled up to the warm, white mound.

Flurries of flakes flittered past, drifting and floating into a lacy lattice curtain which covered the window.

Her eye lids fluttered shut as she drifted back into dreams, her world obscured beneath the white chill.

Fleeting flakes seemed to dwindle into the opaque clouds.

He had not been answering her emails or returning her calls. Just one terse answer-phone message about work commitments.

Finally she broke through and the words tumbled out of her, falling into the vacuum of his pristine white sitting room.

Her legs were spread out on the sofa; lingerie was flung out from the carrier bag and provocatively sprawled across the coffee table.

"Yep," his voice sounded muffled, as though he was shovelling a load of crisps into his mouth.

Sylvie tried to keep her voice light and airy. In the background she could hear a football commentary. "How was your day?"

"Yeah... good." The commentary appeared to have been turned up a little, or else he had moved closer to the television.

"So what have you been doing?"

"Oh… this and that, you know."

Not really she thought, *or I wouldn't be asking.*

"Me too. Just arrived at the chalet. It's not the same without you."

"Uh huh." She could hear cheering in the background.

"Before leaving I thought I'd check up on my Dad to make sure that he would be all right for the next few days."

"Uh huh."

"He set fire to the microwave again."

"Uh huh."

"This time he put his socks into the oven to try to dry them."

"Oh."

"Still, at least he remembered to keep the door shut this time, and the fire brigade know the short cut to his house now."

"Mmmm."

"It's such a shame that you couldn't join me. It has been a year since we've been to the chalet together. I know you've brought some business clients here, but I mean just the two of us, to relax properly." She tried to keep the whine out of her voice.

"Work," he sighed. "You know I can't afford to take the time off."

"Perhaps I should have postponed flying to the chalet?" She paused. "Stayed a bit longer to keep you company?"

Bleary flakes smothered the window and slid slowly downwards.

"Oh no!" he groaned, in unison with the crowd on the television. "No, no, it's fine, you enjoy it." His voice was fast, dismissive.

It was hard to hide the edge of disappointment, to still sound bright, without recrimination, without nagging. "I had been so looking forward to our time alone together." She searched for the usual trigger words, "stockings, steak."

"Yes," he responded, "all good."

It felt like a home goal.

"Tricky," she replied, "with a few hundred miles between us."

"Poor reception," he grunted. "I can't hear you properly."

"Yes," she agreed, "I seem to be losing you."

Sylvie shivered, feeling the cold wind increase as it rattled the windows and sneaked beneath the door. Spinning swirls of snow were whipped up, whirled and flung against the pane.

Fleeting flakes stealthily slunk around the chalet, obliterating the landscape.

She stepped downstairs, surrounded by the resounding silence. The heavy air fell away from her.

Logs collapsed back into the grate, spitting sparks. It felt as though the breath had been punched from inside her, leaving an aching hollowness.

Flames flew up the chimney, casting shadows, whispering secrets. Hidden, yet known.

The mantelpiece mirror threw back the map of her face, refracted in the amber light; each line tracing a new road, the difficult terrain she had crossed, her journey.

Outside the platinum clouds held back the early morning sun rays. Cushions of snow squashed beneath her boots, spongy and squelching.

Slumped backed mountains surrounded her, slumbering beneath their snowy mounds. Pine trees drooped, laden and ready to drop their heavy load.

Sylvie smiled, the wrinkles etched like stars under her eyes. Shivering in the sharp wind stood a small, solitary snowdrop. A mound of snow had parted around the flower, as it waited for the first glimmer of sunlight to break through from behind the mountains.

Little by little, small verdant blotches will seep their way through the snow; tiny islands that will spread and merge.

Soon the mountains would be flooded with a profusion of wild flowers, in rivers of crimson, amber and violet. Tomorrow.

Today she had the nodding snowdrop, alone and lovely. It had broken through the crystalline snow on its slender green stem, hanging its modest white head.

About the author

Linda Flynn has had two humorous novels published: *Hate at First Bite* for 7 – 9 year olds and *My Dad's a Drag*, for teenagers. Both won Best First Chapter in The Writers' Billboard competition.

She has six educational books with the *Heinemann Fiction Project*. In addition she has written for a number of newspapers and magazines, including theatre reviews and several articles on dogs.

Her short stories with Bridge House include: two adult stories, *To Take Flight*, in the *Going Places* anthology and *I knew it in the Bath* in *Something Hidden*, as well as *The Wild Ones*, for teenagers in *Devils, Demons and Werewolves*. Two children's short stories: *The Secret Messenger* and *Timid Tim* were included in *Hippo-Dee-Doo-Dah*.

Linda also works as a Head of English and PR at a school in Middlesex. Her interests include swimming, reading, walking her rescue dogs and far too much time spent daydreaming.

Linda's website is www.lindaflynn.com

Murmuration

L.G. Flannigan

Gwen retrieved the Christmas decorations from the back of the cupboard praying it would keep Fred occupied for at least half an hour before he was yanking at the front door wanting to go out. This need had been manageable a couple of weeks ago when it had been unseasonably warm but now a bitter Arctic wind blew and she was tired of being cold or maybe she was just plain tired.

As Gwen walked into the hall Fred was making a grab for his woolly hat that hung over the newel post at the bottom of the stairs. Nodding to the over flowing box she said, "Fred dear fancy helping me with the Christmas decorations?"

He rolled his eyes. It was his new thing. His way of expressing his dissatisfaction at anything he was unimpressed by. He pulled his hat on. "I want to go out. You can't keep me here."

Gwen kept her sigh inside. It didn't help matters expressing her exasperation. "I know I can't Fred. We're going out in half an hour so help me while you're waiting."

Fred tugged back his jumper sleeve and stared at his watch. He circled its dial with his index finger. It broke Gwen's heart. He'd lost the ability to tell the time over eight months ago.

"It won't take long. I promise." Deliberately she staggered a few steps and tilted the box as if she was about to drop it.

Tutting he said, "Let me take that. Where do you want it?"

It was at times like these, when the old Fred kicked

in, that Gwen had to remind herself that there was no point saying 'in the lounge' as he wouldn't know where that was. "Follow me."

With thoughts of the world outside their front door momentarily forgotten he did as she said placing the box in front of the real Christmas tree that had been delivered yesterday.

Still wearing his hat Fred prodded a branch, "Where did this come from?"

"Bill dropped it off."

He frowned, "Bill? Do I know him?"

"Yes. He owns the grocers in the village."

Fred rolled his eyes and shook his head. "You're wrong. Herb owns the grocers."

He didn't, not anymore, not for thirty years but Gwen knew better than to argue the point. "Of course. What was I thinking?" She forced a smile. She spent most of her time pretending to be wrong to placate him. "He chose well didn't he?"

"Herb's always had a good eye." Fred leant in and sniffed the needles. "I love that smell."

His words warmed Gwen. It was one of his favourite scents. Maybe, just maybe, this would jog his memory for a while. She knelt down and opened the box. "Tinsel first, then the baubles."

"Fairy lights first."

Gwen leant over the box and flicked the plug switch. "I put them on last night."

Fred took a step back and grinned, "I like them. They're new."

They were the same lights they'd had for the last decade but they shone as bright as when they'd first bought them. "They are." She handed him a long piece of tinsel.

His eyes crinkled as he stared at the gold foil

touching his fingers. Gwen took a handful of tinsel and got to her feet. She proceeded to weave it between the branches. Out of the corner of her eye she saw her husband watching her hands. Copying, he put his tinsel on the tree. He surprised her by reaching for more and adding that to the branches.

Gwen picked up the clay stars Fred had made with their three grandchildren five years ago. Last year he had remembered. Dare she hope they may jog his memory. She handed him their granddaughter's star. He traced the indented letters and numbers carved into it with his finger tip. He held the gold thread and tapped it with one finger sending it in a spin.

"Which branch are you going to hang Charlotte's star on?"

Fred frowned, "Charlotte?" He tapped her star again and watched as it continued to rotate. His eyes glazed over and his lips pursed ever so slightly, not enough for anyone else to notice but Gwen knew she had lost him.

"Where's my coat?" The star fell from his fingertips. Gwen caught it just before it hit the oak floorboards.

"In the cloakroom."

The wrinkles round his eyes got deeper, "Cloakroom?"

"I'll show you. You'll need to go to the toilet before you put your coat on." If she was quick she could use the toilet after him and be out before he had finished buttoning his coat. It was always a challenge to be ready before he was rattling the front door. Even though she kept it locked it wasn't good for Fred to get agitated.

Gwen shuddered remembering the last time he'd gone out the front door and disappeared. She'd been haunted by images of him lying in a ditch or being hit by a car. He was missing for three hours and the police had brought home a teary eyed Fred. He was frightened by the whole episode, "You won't let that happen to me again will you? I was scared."

It took a week for the memory of his fear to disappear and then he was back to wanting to go out by himself. Their son Simon bought Fred a watch with a tracking device in it so if he did get lost again she could find him quickly. As a family they agreed it kept Fred safe and that was their priority.

"I'm driving," Fred said. And so begun the five times a day routine of Gwen having to be creative with an excuse so he didn't get cross.

"You can't drive until you've got your new glasses. Remember?"

"Of course I remember. I'm not stupid."

Gwen opened the passenger door for him. He slumped in the seat. Fred hated to be driven, always had.

"Drop me off at the pub. Dad'll be waiting."

In the early days she had gently reminded him that his dad was dead but it would be cruel to do so now. It only distressed him. By the time they drove past the pub at the end of the village high street Fred had forgotten all about meeting his father.

Gwen hoped an outing to the garden centre would hold his attention. It had a large bird feeding section. Fred loved birds. In his middle years he had been a twitcher. Sometimes she'd accompanied him on his hikes into the countryside, rucksacks on their backs and binoculars in hand. It was fun. It had helped with the emptiness they'd both felt when their youngest, Jules, had flown the nest and headed to London to join his brother and sister. Now he lived in Canada and visited once a year.

A corner of their garden was dedicated to birds. Feeders hung from the birch tree and around it Fred had constructed a framework of bamboo canes from which more hung. He would sit in the conservatory watching the birds fly in but over the last two months he'd gradually lost interest.

Someone at the day centre had suggested colourful feeders as Fred, only last week, had admired the ones hanging in their garden. It was worth a try. Anything to fire up his enthusiasm again. He used to say, "The winter is when the birds need us most Gwen."

"This way Fred."

"What are we doing here? This place is all centre and no garden." He chuckled at his joke. The one he'd used for twenty years but not the last two.

It made Gwen nostalgic. Every so often he gave her glimpses of the past and thus clues of what their present, their future may have been like. She swallowed. *No, no tears today.* Instead she smiled, "Very funny dear."

Winking Fred took her hand and squeezed it. If he carried on like that Gwen feared she'd dissolve into tears way before lunch time. Keeping his hand in hers she led him through the vast array of Christmas decorations to the back of the store.

"Why are we here?" Fred's confused frown was back.

"We need some new bird feeders. Some of ours are rusting. Look here, what about these?" Gwen picked up a set of three in traffic light colours.

Fred beamed, "I like them. I, I think someone," he rubbed his brow and his smile faded, "I think I've seen them before, damn why can't I, no it's gone. Damn."

"Never mind Fred. We'll get these and hang them in our garden. Now what feed should we get?"

He shrugged. His interest had evaporated. Quickly Gwen put the brightly coloured wooden house feeders in her basket and grabbed five different feeds. The basket handles dug into the palm of her hand. "This way Fred darling." She watched him as he stared into the distance focussing on nothing in particular. His mind was elsewhere. Maybe she should suggest sitting in the cafe and having a snack before they paid for their items. "Would you like a fresh coffee and a slice of cake Fred?"

His head snapped round. "Chocolate cake?"

"Yes." Gwen prayed that the cafe had some today.

"I'll take that." Fred unpeeled her fingers from the basket handle. That simple act made him feel useful. He pushed back his shoulders and held his head high. Since the disease hit he liked to offer rather than be asked. It had taken Gwen a while to get the hang of that simple differentiation.

Fred raced through his slice of cake and downed his very milky coffee in record time. Gwen liked her coffee black. It never cooled in time for her to drink it before Fred was on his feet wanting to leave. Instead she drank a glass of very unsatisfying orange juice. Refreshing in the summer but not at all a winter warmer.

"Time to go," Fred said.

Gwen picked up the basket and hurried after him grabbing his arm. "Fred, we have to pay. This way."

Confusion etched his face. He didn't recognise her. She continued to smile until he smiled back. It may have been out of etiquette but that smile meant he trusted her. Lifting the basket she said, "We have to pay for this lot."

"Okidoke."

Another one of Fred's little sayings. It seemed random what remained and what memories were irretrievable. And then there were the odd times when a memory she thought he'd lost forever returned and floored her. Only last week, after a year of not being able to, he was back to tying his own shoelaces and moaning, "Why do I have so many awful slip-on shoes? Never liked the buggers."

They were back home less than half an hour before Fred was putting his coat on again. Gwen grabbed a lunch box and shoved in their sandwiches. Resentment wasn't an option. Making the most of what time she had with what was left of her Fred was her priority. Her time to relax would come tomorrow when he went to the day centre.

By the evening they had been out four more times. Dinner had ended up being a microwave meal. Gwen had cooked some frozen vegetables so at least they were getting their greens. She pulled the curtains in the lounge and shut out the world. The cosiness settled Fred. He sat in front of the television surfing the channels. They watched something for ten minutes, sometimes five, before he flicked to the next channel to the extent that Gwen knew solitary facts about a wide range of issues.

The only programme he didn't get bored with was *Strictly Come Dancing* which was strange because it had never interested him before. Not that she was complaining. She liked the banter between the judges, the sparkle and the eye candy. Her neighbour, Vi, was quite taken with this year's obligatory rugby player and with abs like that Gwen wasn't surprised.

The phone rang. Fred got up. He pressed random buttons on the phone, "Hello, hello? Hello? There's no one there."

Gwen held out her hand. Fred wrinkled up his nose and huffed, "There's no one there."

"I know but they may ring back." People usually did now they knew Fred liked to answer. He'd long forgotten how to use a phone. Their eldest son, Simon, had bought one like they used to have in the seventies. Fred was able to use it for a while and then he had forgotten how to use that.

The phone rang again. Gwen looked at the caller ID. It was Jules. "Hi darling."

"Mum, I got cut off."

"I know. How are you?"

"Good, I'm good. Has Si rung you yet?"

"I spoke to him last week."

"Ah, he'll be ringing later then. I beat him to it. We were going to keep this a surprise but Esther said what with Dad being like he is you'd need some warning. Is it all right if I come home for Christmas?"

Gwen blinked away the rapidly forming tears and swallowed.

"Mum, are you there?"

She dabbed her eyes with a tissue, "Yes I'm here. Of course you can come. We'd love that. We haven't had you home for Christmas since, well, for years. When does your flight get in?"

"Early Wednesday. Esther and Tony are picking me up on their way down. We should get to you by one. They're squidging me in the back between the boys."

"That'll be fun."

Jules laughed, "Won't it. I'm sure Si won't mind me warning you. They want to come too but you're not to rush around washing bedding. They'll bring it with them and make up the beds. Will you be all right with a house full?"

Gwen felt like all her Christmases had come at once. Everyone home for Christmas. Tears welled up again.

"Mum?"

"I'll be more than all right."

"Good. Charlotte's going to a sleepover Tuesday so Si said she'll probably be grumpy." Jules snorted. He managed to be an indulgent uncle even though he lived abroad.

"I expect she will be. I'll make her favourite pudding to cheer her up."

"Don't work too hard Mum."

Gwen found herself rolling her eyes like Fred. "I won't."

"Esther and Si worry. They say you're doing too much."

"I know they do."

"We could all stay in a hotel. We weren't sure what to do."

"Honestly I'm fine. I do have my moments, one being the last time I spoke to your sister hence them worrying. But I have listened. I have the cleaner coming in twice a week now and your dad is enjoying the day centre so I've upped his days to three. And Wednesday is one of his days there so I'll have plenty of time to make everyone's favourite foods."

"If you say so. We want to see you though. No hiding away in the kitchen."

"As if. It's big enough for everyone to join me. Simon put in a sofa so you can crash there and watch me."

"We'll all pitch in."

Gwen looked forward to that but even though they were adults she knew from past experience that by the time her children finished with the kitchen it would be like World War III had broken out.

"Mum?" Jules's voice sounded serious.

"Yes."

"We were wondering if Dad might want to go out on Wednesday to watch the starlings come home to roost? I mean it doesn't necessarily have to be that afternoon but Esther said we're all going to the Christingle service on Christmas Eve whether we want to or not so that's Thursday evening out and then we'll probably be slobbing or playing board games on Christmas Day."

Gwen looked across at Fred. He had drifted off, his mouth hung open. He emitted a loud snore. "He's not that interested in birds anymore but it's worth a try. Maybe having everyone here will spark his enthusiasm. Don't get your hopes up though."

"I won't Mum, I promise. I'm sorry I'm not back more to help so are Esther and Si."

"None of you should worry. We have support and neither me nor your father had you so that you'd take care of us."

"I know but—"

"No buts Jules. We're immensely proud of you all. We sort of played a part in that, encouraging you all to follow your dreams. Don't get me wrong we're happy when you get back but we've never had any expectations of that and hey we have Skype."

Jules laughed, "Yes, if you ever turned on the laptop. We all miss you, you know. Just a pity we couldn't all follow our dreams in the same place or drag you and Dad around with us."

Gwen wiped away another tear. How she was holding it together she didn't know. She concentrated on keeping the wobble out of her voice. "Well you know how your dad hates living out of a suitcase so that wouldn't work."

"That's true. So I'll see you in three days."

"I can't wait. Have a safe journey. Love you darling."

"Love you too. Bye."

Gwen rested the phone on her forehead. How many? Esther, Tony and the boys, Harry and Robbie. Jules of course. Simon, Tracey and Charlotte. And with Fred and her that made ten. She hoped they'd been plotting long enough for Esther to have ordered a big enough turkey. Tomorrow she'd order more meat from the butcher. The half decorated tree beckoned her. It could wait for the grandchildren to do but she'd planned to make crackers with Harry and Robbie on Christmas Eve and if Jules could get Fred interested they'd be out Wednesday afternoon.

Making a list in her head Gwen's tiredness was replaced with excitement. All the family home for Christmas. *What more could I want?* Fred snorted momentarily waking himself up. She'd like her husband back but there was little point dwelling on what she couldn't have.

At dusk during the winter months starlings flocked over their house heading for the Levels. It held precious memories for Gwen. The first time they'd driven out to watch the birds swarm in to roost Jules had been a baby. Simon was six and Esther four. Even at that young age they'd been enthralled by it and as enthusiastic as their father.

Gwen and her daughter-in-law Tracey were in the back of Simon's car with Charlotte sandwiched between them. Fred sat in the passenger seat beside Simon. They were like peas in a pod, only Fred's hair was grey and he had more wrinkles. It was a relief not to have to drive and there had been no battle with Fred as it wasn't his car. Despite forgetting he was a father he still recognised his own car.

"Where are we going?"

"To the Levels, Dad, to see the starlings." Simon remained patient even though it was the fifth time he'd said it.

Fred released a long sigh. Although Gwen couldn't see his eyes she knew he'd rolled them.

"I'm meant to be meeting my father at the pub."

"He said to meet him later."

Gwen closed her eyes, content to let Simon take over her responsibility of placating, lying to Fred.

Charlotte rested her head on Gwen's shoulder and whispered, "I miss Grandpops."

Gwen kissed the top of her head, "I know sweetheart, me too." At least he was still with them. Two of her friends weren't so lucky. One had lost her husband to cancer and the other to a heart attack six months before he was due to retire. Fred may remember her infrequently but it was enough. She looked out the window at a turning on the right. "Is that where we used to park Si?"

"Yep," Simon said pulling in.

Fred turned his head and smiled, "Gwen I didn't know you were here."

Her heart lifted. *See these moments are enough.* "I couldn't miss seeing the starlings could I."

His eyes brightened, "We're seeing the starlings?"

"Yes Grandpops," Charlotte said.

"Lottie you're here too. Come and help your old pops out the car."

Charlotte beamed, "Quick Mum get out the way."

Tracey hopped out and Charlotte scrambled across the seat out onto the gravel to open Fred's door. By the time he was standing Charlotte was holding his hand. Harry hurtled from Esther's car to grasp his other.

Simon wrapped his arm round a tearful Gwen and gave her a squeeze. "Jules is choked up too."

She turned to see her other son wiping his eyes and held out her hand. He rushed over, quickly followed by Esther. Gwen found herself in the middle of a hug with all three of her children. Anxious not to crumble into a blubbering wreck she cleared her throat and said, "I love you all very much but there's no time for dawdling. It'll be dark soon."

Already prepared for the puddles and mud in their wellies the group traipsed across the narrow country road to a well beaten track onto the Levels joining the steady stream of visitors. Simon led the way with Robbie. Gwen, Esther and Tracey brought up the rear while Jules walked with Tony, Fred, Charlotte and Harry.

"Where are you leading us boy?" Fred called out to Simon.

"Just our usual place, Dad."

"I've never been here before," Fred grumbled looking left to right at the wetlands. "There's not much to see."

Charlotte looked over her shoulder a frown marring her face.

Gwen gave her an encouraging nod, "You're doing good."

Tight lipped she shrugged.

"It must be hard dealing with Dad day in day out, Mum." Hands shoved in her coat pockets Esther kicked at a stone.

"It can be but I have help and as long as I don't get too tired it's not too bad. There are people worse off than me."

"You have the patience of a saint. I'm not sure I could manage twenty four seven," Tracey said.

"You would dear. I'm not saying I don't have my moments where I have to count to ten sometimes a hundred but if you love someone you just take a deep breath and carry on. Getting cross would only agitate him."

The ground became boggier as they neared the large reed bed and the gathering of people already there to watch the starlings too.

"Let's stop here," Simon said with Esther's youngest Robbie on his shoulders. His mud covered wellies smeared his uncle's coat.

"I'm so sorry Si," Esther said rubbing at it.

"No worries. Let it dry, it'll brush off later."

"Look, look!" Harry pointed skyward as dusk rolled in.

A hum of appreciation rippled through the watchers. In the distance there was what seemed like a never ending stream of black dots heading towards them, forming dark swaying clouds overhead. Everyone was quiet. It heralded the start of something spectacular. More starlings swooped in adding to the black mass. The huge cloud wheeled to the left, and just as suddenly turned to the right, their collective movement a breathtaking acrobatic aerial display.

"Lottie, Lottie, look it's a, oh what's the darn word? Gwen, where's my Gwen she'll know." Fred swivelled his head in Gwen's direction.

Gwen let go of her daughter's hand and joined her granddaughters and her old Fred determined to make the most of his fragile hold on his memory of her.

"Look Gwen, it's a murmuration."

Gwen hugged him. "I'd forgotten what it was called."

"Dad, it's called a murmuration, Grandpops said."

Simon moved closer to Charlotte, "So it is. Well done Dad."

Staring up at the sky they all huddled closer with Gwen and Fred in the middle. Gwen had never felt more loved and supported.

"Why do they call it a murmuration, Grandpops?" Harry said.

Fred frowned at his grandson, his eyes darting back and forth. Gwen knew he was struggling to understand who it was asking the question. He gave up trying to figure it out and instead cupped his ear, "Can you hear that lad?"

The whole family followed his lead and cupped their ears. The flock wheeled again and split in two creating what looked like a giant winged bird. "Hear that murmur."

"Yes." Harry clapped his gloved hands together.

"It's their wings."

The split flock re-joined and wheeled again creating what looked like a pulsating jellyfish.

"Amazing," Fred said kissing Gwen on the cheek. Her skin tingled. It was going to be a good Christmas.

"Thank you," she mouthed to her children. They smiled back at her.

"Grandma look!" Charlotte held out her hand as a snowflake landed in her palm and melted. It was followed by another and another. It was years since they'd had a white Christmas. Her family was all together. Yes this year it was going to be a good loving Christmas indeed.

Dedication
Dedicated to people whose lives are affected by dementia including my wonderful parents.

About the author
L.G. Flannigan loves dark chocolate and her children, husband and dog. She lives in Somerset and when not writing works in a library. She writes contemporary adult and young adult novels plus the occasional short story, and was previously published in the *On This Day* anthology. Her contemporary novel *Ordering Flynn Matthews* was recently shortlisted in Choc-Lit's 'Search for a Star Competition'. L.G.'s infrequent musings can be found at http://lgflannigan.wordpress.com.

The Meetings

Paula R. C. Readman

As I sit on the park bench, I trace out the words engraved on the small metal plaque with my fingertips. By doing this simple act, I recall the happiness I witnessed so long ago.

Every day I come here as he did, all those years ago, and wondered if the plaque could be a marker for my life too. As crazy as it may seem I used to watch him, this unknown person, so strong, so full of life, and her too.

I noticed the young woman first. Usually, she came into the park, where I worked from a small, side-road. Her long, blonde hair flowed behind her like a veil of sunshine, even on the dullest of days; her footfall on the gravel was so light it barely made a sound.

Some days when I was busy tidying the flowerbeds, I would almost miss her arrival. Straightening up to ease my back, I would catch sight of her pausing in the gateway. Her face would brighten when she saw him. Laughing, she would rush into his waiting arms.

The casually, dressed man would arrive at the park some mornings so early; the mist hadn't had time to clear to wait for her. He was always the first to arrive and came into the park through the main entrance, with its large ornate gates of black and gold. A couple of hours later, she would arrive with her beautiful smile.

I never quite knew what time of day they would arrive. Sometimes, if the weather was awful in the morning, they came in the afternoon, but I never saw the two of them arrive together.

At first, I wasn't sure about their relationship, whether they were lovers or not. Not that it was any of my business. I just saw two happy people enjoying each other's company.

Happiness is a rare thing these days and I considered myself the lucky one, a silent witness to the happiness they shared as I worked among the flowerbeds and borders.

I've never been a good judge of age, but I thought the man looked slightly older than the woman as the sun highlighted the passing of his years in the changing colour of his hair. Though to be truthful, I didn't like to guess the woman's age as I hadn't seen her close up, well, not at first.

They used to stroll leisurely around the park, arm in arm. The woman gazed intensively at the man's face as though she'd never tire of it. Occasionally, I would stumble across them standing close together down by the fountain or up on the rise overlooking the town.

He with his arm around her narrow waist, talking to her in his easy, gentle way while studying something of interest like the multitude of colourful butterflies feeding restlessly on the globe buddleia bush.

Sometimes, as if by magic, the man would produce a bag of bread. The young woman's laughter would fill the air as she wiped at her eyes before hugging his neck. Together like children, they would race along the path to the pond. I would hear her gentle voice carried on the light summer breeze calling back to him to hurry up.

Down at the pond, the swans were the first to know there was food on offer. They would swim over with their haughty looks as the woman attempted to throw the bread to them, but the smaller, more agile, comical ducks would get in first. Together, the couple would laugh at the antics of the swans and ducks until all the bread had gone.

On another day as I trundled about with my wheelbarrow moving from flowerbeds to borders, I came across them,

154

sitting with their heads intimately close together.

Like me, they were especially fond of the bench under the spreading oak tree on a rise overlooking the town. On one occasion as I dug out the flowerbed, ready for the seasons planting, I watched the man produce a bag of nuts. The unexpected look of pure pleasure that crossed the woman's face was a remarkable sight.

As though by some supernatural power from nowhere squirrels appeared, and came down from the branches above her to feed on the nuts she held out.

Its seemed to me, the man brought a sort of enchantment into the woman's life; I know he did to mine. I began to look forward to their visits, to share unknowingly in their happiness.

It makes me smile even now, as I remembered sharing in birthdays and Christmas celebrations on this bench. He was like a magician conjuring brightly coloured balloons, and ribbons out of nowhere to decorate it before she arrived.

As she came up the rise towards him, he produced a cake with lit candles. Once she was seated, he'd arranged her long, flowing, bohemian skirt around her sandaled feet, and then set up his camera he'd photograph them together while she blew out the candles.

The autumn seemed to arrive quite quickly that last year. You could smell the change of seasons in the air. I'd only just unlocked the park gates when the man appeared out of the early morning mist.

He walked much slower now, a little unsteadily and with the aid of a stick. He seemed a little embarrassed to see me, and nodded his acknowledgment before turning away to make a slow progress up the slight rise to wait as he always did on their bench beneath the oak tree.

I felt foolish and embarrassed at showing my shock

at the sudden change in him and quickly, I turned my attention back to raking the first of the falling leaves.

As the weeks flew by there were too many jobs needing to be done to notice their absence from the park. As the flowering season ended, I began clearing the flowerbeds and borders, deadheading the roses, cutting back the shrubs and splitting some of the large plants to make new ones. While tidying the edge of the pond and pulling out some of the invasive weeds, my mind was already planning next spring's planting as I made lists of bulbs I needed to order. I cleared the flowerbeds and borders ready for next spring's season planting. Soon the day came when the first snow of the season began to fall. I hurried along the path to my park keeper's hut and was shocked to find the young woman sitting alone, her face and hands as white as the snow at her feet.

Sobbing softly, she stood up when she saw me. Smiling weakly, she greeted me like an old friend and held out a small, brightly coloured parcel. The words tumbled from her in between uncontrollable sobs as she tried to ask me something.

Unlocking my hut, I asked her to step in out of the cold, so she could take her time explaining to me what she wanted.

The warmth that hit us added colour to her cheeks and hands. I gestured to her to sit on an old park bench I had just finished repairing, while I waited for the kettle to boil to make us both a hot drink. As we waited, I was able to study her face for the first time and noticed the fine lines around her sad eyes.

On taking the mug of hot tea, she began explaining what she had tried to tell me.

The gentleman had passed away about a month ago and she could not face coming to their special place until now. Picking up the carefully wrapped object, she passed it to me.

With tears in her large brown eyes, she asked if it would be possible to fit the small plaque to the bench beneath the old oak tree.

On opening the object, I stared at it unable to speak.

Her sad face broke into a gentle smile at the shock that must have registered on my face. He was her father she began to explain. They had found each other after years of being apart. It was only after her mother had passed away, she'd been able to search for him. He had promised her he would make up for all their lost years, so they had spent their time together flying kites, visiting the zoo, and building sandcastles on the beach, but most of their meetings, they spent enjoying the park as this was the last place she had remembered him bringing her to as a small child.

She told me her father had remarried, but they had been unable to have children of their own, so he had kept his lost daughter a secret, wishing only to protect them both.

It was only when he'd become too ill to come to the park that he had told his wife about her. With tears rolling down her cheeks, she explained how his wife had phoned her, begging her to come to the hospital.

Together, they had sat at his side, sharing his last moments together. After taking a sip of tea, she carried on explaining.

Now her stepmother and she had become good friends and she spent most her free time visiting her as often as she could. Her greatest wish was to have something in the park to remind her of the wonderful times she had spent with her lost father, and to remind other people of their fathers too.

I nodded and picked up my screwdriver. Together we stepped out into the snow and made our way to the rise. As we fastened the last screw into the plaque, she read the words aloud:

'In memory of all the lost fathers; may one day your children come back into your lives to play for awhile.'

As I watched her walk away that day, I became aware our footprints were the only ones in the freshly fallen snow and suddenly I recalled the happy times I had spent with my father playing on my sledge on sunny winter's days so long ago.

And as I sit here now, it reminds me of all the joy I've shared with my own children and grandchildren too.

About the author
Paula R. C. Readman lives in Essex. In 2010, her first success was with English Heritage, who selected her story for *Whitby Abbey – Pure Inspiration*. Since then she's had several other short stories published and won two writing competitions. In 2011, *The Meetings* was selected the overall winner by Austin Macauley in their short story competition. In 2012, *Roofscapes* was selected as the overall winner by best-selling crime writer Mark Billingham in the Harrogate Crime writing Festival. In 2015 Parthian Books selected one of her stories for their New Gothic Fiction: *A Flock of Shadows*. Now she's working hard to find a home for her first novel.

Find out more about Paula and her writing on her Amazon Author page or on her blog
http://paulareadman1wordpress.com

Eight Hours Going Nowhere

Sarah Evans

Hour zero

Luka grits his teeth against the night air as he drops down from the cab of the lorry. Hitching was slow tonight and he needs to be brisk as he walks across the frosted tarmac towards the back-entrance doors marked *staff*. The doorway smells of piss, diesel and fag-ends. He types in the joke of a security code. *1234.* The blast of heated air comes as a relief, but only temporarily. The place stinks of citrus floor cleaner and already he is starting to feel hot, his skin clammy, his face desiccated.

He opens his locker, drags out the plastic-feel tunic and peaked cap that form his uniform and shoves his jacket and rucksack in. He reports to the manager on duty, then makes his way towards the food court, taking his place behind the counter.

It is midnight, hour zero, the start of his eight hour shift. *Alena*, he thinks, *I am doing this for you.*

Hour one

He's been here for nearly an hour now and the food in hot trays has been there much longer. Heat rises from the metal surfaces along with stench of burnt oil, stale fish and onion gravy. People come and go, in through the entrance doors, out the exits, transiting this nowhere place. Custom has been intermittent. Slow, slow; fast, fast; slow. Endless minutes tick by with nothing for him to do other than occasionally running through the chips or peas with a slotted spoon, redistributing moisture. Then all of a sudden there will be a rush, with half a dozen people

159

expecting that he can grow octopus arms and serve them all simultaneously.

A couple of trucker types are approaching, guys with pregnant bellies and arms the girth of a thigh, the exposed skin covered in intricate tattoos.

He stirs the pot of gravy which has thickened to the consistency of snow-sludge.

"This all there is?" one of men asks, gesturing the spaces between the trays.

"It is the night-time menu we are serving now." Luka has practised this sentence out loud, over and over in the tiny room he co-rents with someone who works day-light hours. It never sounds quite how he would like it to.

The two men exchange a glance, bristling at the sound of him. *Bloody immigrants.* He'd like to protest that he has entered the country legally, is here because of the bits of paper that the elected government of the United Kingdom has freely signed, and because no one born here wants to work in a place like this.

He knows as he dishes it up that the battered fish will be soggy and the chips will taste of cardboard. The overpriced, substandard food is not his fault. His place is simply to serve.

The man prods the fish with a stubby finger. "Bleeding cold," he says.

Luka looks back neutrally. He offers to put it in the microwave, aware that doing so will remove whatever remaining texture there might be.

The customer doesn't want it *f-ing* microwaved; he wants it fresh. Luka holds himself tight, keeping his surface-self polite and calm as he says he is very sorry but this is all there is. The customer kicks the counter and he keeps cursing. Luka's fingers inch towards the red panic button concealed beneath the work-top. *For emergencies*

160

only. Eventually the truckers move onwards towards the tills. Luka remembers too late that he should have said *have a nice day*, or *evening*, or – in this case – *night*. He runs his slotted spoon through the boiled-to-oblivion peas. He thinks of Alena standing at the stove, raising a wooden spoon to her lips, conjuring a wholesome feast from leftovers. Once he has covered the basics of rent and food, he has nothing but scraps left. *I'll send money as soon as I can.*

He is one hour down and an eternity to go.

Hour two

Trade has slowed even further. Staff have been reduced to a skeleton, none of them fully alive, all of them with hopes that got trampled on somewhere along the way.

A mobile rings. Not his. He should ring Alena. His phone is inside his uniform, pressed against his heart. He thinks how the sound of her voice would lift his day, or rather night. She'll be asleep, of course, the difference in time-zone not long, the distance between them much further. He thinks of her hair spreading over the pillow, of the way one arm will be curled behind her head, of the peaceful rhythm to her breathing.

With no customers in view, he is free to dream. Being here, this job, it's a gateway to somewhere better, the first step that will open the door to grander things. In his mind he is explaining that to Alena. If he didn't believe this, he doesn't know how he'd get himself up in the evening, how he'd make it through the night.

Hour three

These hours are the dead hours, the blank time between those travelling late and those travelling early. The food is shrivelled beyond recognition, but the trays remain to justify the claim of 24-hour service. He is being paid to stand and stare into nothing, time moving so slowly it seems almost to come to a stop. The advert said they wanted people who were customer focussed and dynamic; what they need is workers who won't go insane with boredom.

He sees movement. A woman has stopped on the threshold of the open-plan space. Her gaze skims over Luka and he feels like raising a hand in greeting, because he recognises her as one of those rare things: a regular. But her eyes have already moved on and she is walking towards one of the tables on the very edge.

He ought to go and remind her that tables are for customers only. As if it could possibly matter.

He wipes down the surfaces of the counter that he wiped just five minutes ago. He feels his body shift into high alert as if he was the one anticipating a grand entrance. He watches this drably dressed middle-aged woman sitting upright on the plastic chair, her hands clasped before her on the table.

Even though he has been waiting, the moment catches him unawares; the man is there, materialising out of the stale air. His hair is grey, his face etched with weariness, but he gains animation within the sphere of the woman he comes here once a week to meet.

Luka wonders what other lives they lead, why it is that night-time is the only time they have. Wonders why they don't book an anonymous room in the adjoining hotel, choosing instead this public place. To talk. Or not talk, just looking into each other's eyes and holding hands. He bursts to tell them that life is short and you only have the one shot at getting the performance right, and whatever disruptions they might leave behind, surely in the long run it will be worth it. Grasp the beautiful moment, because it may never come again.

162

Alena. Her name stabs him, over and over during the quiet, witching hours. He tries not to think about the last time he saw her, the time they both said things they didn't mean, not really. Her accusations rained down like arrows, her telling him that he was a waste of space and time, with his lack of work, lack of skills, lack of money. How could he hope to support a family? And him knowing she was right, only it wasn't his fault and wasn't fair for her to keep on at him like that. She didn't necessarily mean for him to up and leave, he knows that. Just as he knows that he should ring her, but he can't, not yet. He will do. Soon. Just needs to get himself established, to find his feet, as if they aren't right there at the end of his long legs, encased in trainers which are splitting apart.

The couple stand; they clasp one another as if this is their last leaving, though likely they'll be back in a week's time, stuck within their hope and despair.

Hour four

The eye-lid drooping tedium is shattered by the approaching cluster of chattering, laughing women. *Working girls. Ladies of the night.* He doesn't like to use some of the harsher words he's learned. He's seen them before, or perhaps their type all look the same. The same bleached hair. Same ruby lipstick and the reek of astringent perfume which covers up who knows what. The high heels and short tight skirts and low cut tops even though it's sub-zero out there. The same optical illusion so that – from a distance – they have a feminine allure, but up close it's clear they're older, tireder, more used and worn looking than you initially thought.

"Three teas," one of them says.

"The machine is there," he replies. "Please help yourself."

She looks at him like he's nothing, like she's way, way above him, despite her doing what she does.

"Cups to the side," he adds, though it's pretty obvious. Her glossy mouth pouts and he thinks of the things those lips might do; he tries to think of something else. They talk amongst themselves in their language and he understands some of the words, but he doesn't want to make that kind of connection.

He rings up the three teas and three packets of sugary biscuits on the till. At this time of night, he's one half of a duo and his other half is off having a piss, though he's taking a mighty long time about it.

The ladies, girls whatever he's to call them, commandeer a table in the centre, preening themselves like parakeets. One of them stretches back, her hand placed over the small mound of her belly, making him wonder... *Surely not.*

He's seen these girls at work before, when he's taking a fag break, girls doing the rounds, heading for the outer reaches of the lorry park, going vehicle to vehicle, banging on the doors. He thinks of those bruiser guys earlier and how the girls/ladies always seem so slight and the thoughts fill him with a mix of pity and revulsion. The girls are likely tough. They operate in small groups, one girl keeping watch, one eye out for security, the other for any signs of trouble from the client. He can picture the way they fidget on their high heels, shifting to keep their balance, the tips sticking in the urine-coated tarmac.

Desire stirs despite himself, despite the fact that he doesn't want – not really – this type of woman, that kind of transaction, sex reduced to the precise things he can and cannot do within an allotted number of minutes. He couldn't afford it anyway. Just it's been a long time. Thoughts of Alena press, provoking an ache of loneliness.

164

The women leave and everything reverts to calm. To the stultifying boredom of the night-shift.

Hour five

He's past the halfway mark and it's his turn now to take a bit of a break though he's not supposed to be gone for more than ten minutes.

He heads towards the loos. The staff toilets are cleaned less regularly than the customer ones so he uses the latter which smell of pink cleaning fluid and where condom machines sit alongside ads for erectile-dysfunction treatment.

Afterwards, he goes up towards the enclosed bridge that straddles the services between this side and the other, though it hardly seems to justify its existence. Not like the facilities are any different. Not much use for vehicle owners. It allows a hitcher like himself to perform a U-turn, to change his mind about the direction taken. He thinks of Alena trying to persuade him to come back home. *Come home to me, Luka. To us.*

Through the smeared window, snowflakes are gently drifting, lit up by the moving headlamps below. Red lights recede on one side of the road while yellow ones race towards him on the other. Standing in the middle of the bridge, life rushing beneath, he feels like he's standing at the pivot of the world; he's everywhere and nowhere.

Hour six

Trade picks up now as they move onto breakfast. The chef is here and full flow. Luka hoists empty trays out-back and hot, heavy ones out-front. Mounds of pale, freshly cooked chips. Curls of fatty bacon. Rows of egg-eyes and a slosh of beans.

He serves and smiles, smiles and serves and wishes

everyone *a good day*. The old and young. The loners, couples and families. A trio arrives, the parents' clothes crumpled, the baby clothed in soft pink, her face red and cross.

Yes, he can warm up baby food, it's not a problem. The microwave pings after just a few seconds and the air fills with baked banana and honey; it smells of childhood and of home. The woman's smile is warm and open. "Thank-you so much." Her gratitude is out of all proportion and something inside him swells with fellow feeling.

He thinks of the baby growing inside Alena, the random chance of a life beginning. He thinks of her threats to get rid of it, because after all how were they going to feed a child, clothe it and protect it. It's one of the reasons he hasn't dared to ring, not knowing how to ask, still not having – not really – an answer to those questions. The money he's saved in his weeks here, it seems so insubstantial.

The family take a table close to the counter. The baby has settled and is offering her mother a squirrel-cheeked smile as the young woman spoons in the baby mush. "Da, da, da," the baby chants between mouthfuls, her hands waving uncoordinatedly with the excitement of being alive. "Da, da, da." And it's just a sound, but he sees the way the father's face lights up, the soft look between him and the woman. He sees the tight boundedness of the three of them.

"You serving or what?" The voice is harsh and returns Luka to himself and to his unending night.

Hour seven

Time speeds up; the last hour passes in a flash of serving spoons and constant clink of plates. So many people, all wanting piles of oil-slicked food.

166

Time is ticking down. The working girls are back – more tea and biscuits – and they look expended, their lipstick smeared; they are out of place amongst the families, lone travellers and truckers. The different groups pretend not to notice one another, their lives moving forward on parallel lines.

Alena showed him the test, the twin blue lines that held the possibility of their future.

Time freeze-frames and all of life is snapped: love and lust, grief and joy, regrets and hopes, ugliness and beauty.

Hour eight

Luka is free, finally, to head for the exit. His limbs are heavy as if they obey a different force of gravity. He wriggles out of his tunic, shoves it in the locker then heads over the bridge. The other side, he emerges into the diesel-fresh air of early morning. A thin layer of snow crunches beneath his feet. The sun is rising, a great orange smudge against the sky, glinting off the whiteness which has settled, turning the world clean and fresh. He feels the uplift provided by the sun's splendour, even here against the backdrop of concrete buildings and the hornet-drone of the motorway. The lorry park is moving, the overnight kippers moving onwards and hopefully someone will give him a lift where he needs to go.

He takes his phone out of his pocket. He put £5 worth of credit on, though he has no idea how many minutes that might buy him. He needs to ring Alena. He should have done it before, but each day it gets a little harder and if he doesn't do it soon he never will.

He needs to do it now. *Now!* He wants to tell her how life is beautiful and brutal. How it is short. So many things to tell her, but he doesn't know if he can find the words.

After eight hours amongst the almost dead, he feels himself bursting with aliveness. If she kept the child it will be showing, her belly starting to puff out, round and firm. He thinks of those women and how despite everything they laugh and chat, the warmth spreading between them. Of the rose-petal blush of the baby's cheeks, and her staccato *da, da, da*. Of the couple who meet here once a week in the middle of the night and all the other lonely, unhappy souls passing by. He feels the accumulative force of chance impressions, nudging the neural pathways in his brain.

A snowflake settles on his cheek and melts.

Grasp the moment.

He presses the button on his phone, his heart battering as if the button was for emergencies only. He holds himself like steel, forcing himself to clutch the wedge of metal to his ear as he listens to the ring. Within the pause, he thinks of the baby hovering in the nowhere land of existence or not, and how by asking, he will make whatever has happened real, summoning the child into being or condemning it to oblivion, a baby's life oscillating over electromagnetic waves. He hears the click of the pick-up and his whole body snaps alert.

"Alena," he says. "It is me."

About the author

Sarah Evans has had over a hundred stories published in anthologies, magazines and online. Highlights include: appearing in the 2008 Bridport anthology; having several stories published in the acclaimed *Unthology* series (Unthank Books); recently winning the inaugural Winston Fletcher Prize with her story *Acclimatising*. She's also had work published by Bloomsbury, Fiction Desk, Bridge House Publishing and Rubery Press, and performed live in London, Hong Kong and New York.

Buster Blizzard

Steve Wade

White. Everything was white.

The children collected what they needed from their mothers' kitchens. Up they trooped to the top of the road that overlooked the valley. Here, beneath the shelter of the Hanging Tree, they got to work.

It was here, the previous Christmas, the father of one of the children had been found dead.

They compacted the soft snow into three parts. With these they formed his legs, his torso and his head. Two black olives they inserted as his eyes, for his mouth a half-moon of coffee beans, and for his nose, a carrot. His arms they fashioned from long twigs, on whose ends they put a pair of mittens. And lastly, upon his head they placed a ring of holly with red berries. This was Joshua's idea. The youngest of the pals. It was Joshua's father's lifeless body that had been found hanging from the tree the previous Christmas. Buster Blizzard, the name they always gave him, was complete.

Around their creation they danced and laughed until creeping darkness scared them and they ran home. All except Josh, who stayed with Buster Blizzard so the snowman wouldn't be alone in the scary darkness. Besides, Josh's mom was still in work, and he didn't like being by himself since his daddy left them. He moved in close to the tree for shelter.

Daylight, pure and bright, slunk off at the approach of her shadowy stalker the Night. The realization that the kingdom of Snowtopia would soon awake came to Buster Blizzard as a fuzzy feeling. The previous year, Snowtopia, like Buster Blizzard, had lain dormant.

The snowman, the king of Snowtopia, trembled at the consequences of his absence. Without their yearly period of respite in Snowtopia, the world of mortals would have forgotten its humanity. And the birds and animals, too, would have been corrupted. Perhaps he was already too late.

Silence, no sound save for the far-off whispering of a million tiny voices told the snowman king his loyal army was on its way.

From the skies they fell, a myriad of snowflakes. Into his ears they whispered confirmation of his fears. Mortal mothers and fathers, they told him, had neglected their parental duties. Instead of bonding with their children last Christmas, they'd abandoned them, left them with nannies and child-minders so that they were free to make merry in public houses.

The king lowered his head, his dark-eyed gaze locked to his own blue shadow. But he looked up quickly when a robin landed on his outstretched arm.

"Ah, my little friend. Good to see you're still thriving."

The robin hopped onto the king's shoulder. "Sire. For eight seasons I have awaited your return. I have much to report."

"So. How fare the birds and beasts?"

The robin broke into a sweet melody that told Buster Blizzard of the changes his absence had wrought upon the animal kingdom. The bird sang of how Winter, the goodly white giant, confused when the snow-king failed to greet his arrival the year before, departed hurriedly. The little bird sang too of how the goddess Spring came early. And following her the buzzing of a billion wing-beats. The bees pollinated the flowers that had bloomed too soon. And so formed seed and berries that swelled beneath

170

Spring's tender touch.

In their thousands they came, the Scandinavian winter visitors, ravenous flocks of redwings and fieldfares. But they were too late. Stripped of winter food supplies, the land offered no sustenance. A deadly change came over these winter migrants. Those that rejected the change in diet from fruits and seeds to flesh and blood succumbed to Mac Tire, a wolf known to all the birds and mammals as the Black Beast. Death.

As he listened to the robin's tale, the red berries in Buster Blizzard's holly crown began to melt. He wept crimson tears.

A voice, unknown to the snowman king, speaking from within the tree, refocused his attention.

"My son Josh. You've got to help him. The cold has put him to sleep. He's freezing to death."

As familiar with and fearless of the dead as he was the not-yet-dead, Buster Blizzard summoned his second in command, the North wind. A feisty old fellow, he appeared from nowhere.

"Quick," Buster Blizzard said. "Carry to the boy's mother his father's words."

The North Wind sucked in his cheeks and with them the plea from the silhouetted figure dangling from a rope above. And with that the old man sprinted off down the hill, and to the factory where the boy's mother was working late.

Another surprise awaited the snowman king. Talk of death had lured from the shadows a creature with amber eyes: Mac Tire. The dark wolf skulked forward towards the tree to where lay the boy called Josh.

"No," the king said. "It's not his time."

The great wolf turned his pointy muzzle to the king, his jaws open in a canine smile. His tongue he drew across his lips. First Mac Tire licked the boy's neck, and then his face, until Josh made audible breathing sounds.

"You are a noble creature," the snowman king said. "Sometimes all of us, mortal or immortal, are as blinded by mythology as we are in a whiteout.

Another voice, a woman's, calling out turned the heads of snow, feather and fur alike. That old lank grey hair, the North Wind. Back already. From his toothless and gaping mouth came the boy's mother's voice.

At the far end of the whitened street came the voice's real owner.

"Sylvia," a strangled voice called from the branches overhead.

The snowman king craned his neck as the voice called again his wife's name, his words sounding as though a pair of huge hands were wrapped about his neck, her name choking in his throat. The silhouette of the hanging man than grew faint and disappeared.

"Help her," Buster Blizzard commanded the North Wind.

In a huge leap, the old man was next to her. He took her by the hand and helped her climb the icy incline. The birds and beasts melded into the shadows on her arrival.

"Josh," she said, with outstretched arms. "My baby. Josh."

The boy awoke as though from a dream-filled slumber. He smiled at her a smile so bright and filled with the greatest love that exists: the love that bonds a mother and a child.

From the surrounding bushes and shadows there began a chorus of chirrups, whistles, hoots, grunts, clucks and cackles. A sound so wondrous, so sublime, parents and children, from the warmth of their homes in the valley below, pulled back curtains and opened blinds. And they watched through lighted windows the swirling snowflakes dancing and spiralling from the sky. Perfect. Christmas as it should be; Christmas, a time for families to be together, to stay indoors, to share stories, to play games, to reconnect through laughter, fun, and magic.

The snowman king, from the top of the hill that overlooked his kingdom, Snowtopia, closed his eyes, exhausted yet elated that his arrival hadn't, after all, been too late. And he dreamt. For even snowmen find time to dream.

About the author

Steve Wade is a prize nominee for the PEN/O'Henry Award, 2011, and the Pushcart Prize, 2013. His fiction has won awards and been placed in prestigious writing competitions. His novel, *On Hikers' Hill* was awarded First Prize in the UK abook2read Literary Competition, December 2010 – the British lyricist sir Tim Rice was the top judge.

www.stephenwade.ie

Episode

L F Roth

There is no beginning. I am simply there, looking at the man beside the taxi. It is no one I recognize. The back door is open. Another man is lying on the seat, his feet sticking out. That is my father.

The stranger's voice is slurred.

"You take his legs."

I hesitate. "What's wrong with him?"

"You could say he's had one too many."

"You from his office?"

"Nah. His lodge."

I don't know what a lodge is.

"He'll tell you. How old are you?"

"Eleven."

"Will you manage? Your mother looked stronger."

I shrug. "I'll manage."

I do, but I have to rest on each landing.

And that is it. Not only is there no beginning – there is no ending either. It is as if I had abandoned my father on the top landing, outside the flat where we lived, the four of us, my mother, father, younger brother and I, forever excluded, no longer part of my life.

Now, years later, I can supply some of what is missing. Although it left no imprint, my father must have been home to dress for the event, his first appearance, perhaps the only one, at some lodge, which in all likelihood took the form of an initiation ceremony. By bedtime, that is, my bedtime, he was probably already nearing the limit of what he could take. Another glass or two of whatever he was having would have put him out. He wasn't that much of a drinker.

174

But the lack of a proper beginning bothers me. The man who brought my father home must have come to the door – how else would he have known that my mother looked stronger than me? What had he said? *Your husband's outside in a cab. He's out cold. You'll have to give me a hand.* Would that have been it? And what had been her reaction? Had she been angry? Upset? Disgusted? I just don't know. Neither the next day nor at some later point did she so much as allude to the incident. The fact that she didn't go down herself but sent me suggests that she wanted to have nothing to do with it. Nor can I recall what words she used when she came to wake me. They would have constituted a command and not a plea, of that I am sure: *You have to get dressed. Your father needs help* – the reference would be to 'Your father' even at that point, not Dad or Daddy. But this is pure speculation. You would expect something so out of the ordinary to remain imprinted on my mind in all its details, but there is nothing there except the taxi and the slow climb up the stairs.

My father didn't talk about it either. For all I know, he may never have learned who carried him upstairs.

The two of them must have talked, though, husband and wife. My father must have come to with few if any recollections of the night before, presumably still fully dressed unless my mother had taken care to remove his shoes. He would have looked around, confused, the sharp light hurting his eyes, his head pounding, and found himself, where? On the living-room couch? In their bedroom? My mother would have been nowhere around. He would have got up awkwardly and gone to look for her. And there I have to end all speculation: what took place between them is part of a story I didn't get to hear. In fact, all of that morning is a blank. In the months that

175

followed, my father slept in the living room as often as not; the explanation that I didn't ask for was that the bedroom was too warm. But that first morning left no echo in my mind of angry voices, nor the oppressive weight of suffocating silences. There is nothing.

There is nothing until late in the afternoon. "Would you two like to go to the cinema?" my mother asked. "Would you, Geoffrey? Peter?" Of course we would, my brother and I. "Right," she said. "Tell your father I'm taking you." When I realized he was to be excluded, I hesitated, momentarily, but Peter, for whom this would be the first time ever, shouted: "Daddy! Mummy's taking us to the pictures!" without any attempt from her to stop him from yelling, as she would have done in normal circumstances.

Pictures for punishment. The treat that only I had experienced until that day, reserved for special occasions, had been changed into its opposite, not for me but for my father, the one who had taken me the few times I had been, while Peter, five years younger, had had to stay at home. There weren't many films suitable for both of us.

Star Wars was, my mother had decided. She read the title and the brief introduction aloud for Peter's benefit as the film started; I pointed out that the number was wrong: it should be *Episode I*, not *IV*. Eleven-year-olds are such know-it-alls. Now, at forty-eight, I can account for the numbering of the *Star Wars* sequence, but I am less sure of myself in other areas. For one thing, memory, I have learned, tends to play tricks on you.

Mostly, of course, what happens leaves no trace at all: so little is retained. That is the case with the first few years of my life; I recall hardly anything until I was five. That must be when the photo was taken – the photo that came in the post and brought to mind, again, the night and the afternoon I would as soon forget; the man, the taxi, the trudge up the stairs; the bitter treat. The photo itself holds no memories. It is one I haven't seen before. It is of a scene that I don't recognize. In it, my father is sitting on the ground, leaning against a wall; I am standing beside him. We are both squinting into the sun. The shadow cast by the photographer reaches my father's feet. I assume it is my mother's, but there is no telling; the compressed dark shape has no traits by which it can be identified. There is no Peter. "Thought you might want this," says the note that was enclosed with it. "Your Dad."

If the picture was to have a caption, it should read 'Father and son', I decide. Or maybe not – why state the obvious? 'At the seaside' would be a better choice. There is no sea, but the wall, whitewashed, rough, is of the type that separates roads or car parks from the beach in many places. I am wearing shorts and a T-shirt, my father, always the businessman, plain grey trousers and a light blue and white striped shirt, the button-down collar and the absence of jacket and tie his only concession to the setting. Neither of us will go swimming, I am certain, though the season may be right.

Are we happy? It is hard to tell. The photo is as sharp as can be expected of one taken, presumably, with a cheap camera, but there are necessarily few details: it is the standard size print produced by the shops in those days. If neither of us is laughing, nor do we look sad. We are close but not touching. The scene has a generic quality: there is nothing to suggest that the same photo couldn't be taken again and again for many years to come, father and son together, symbolically protected by the wall behind us from anything that might pose a threat.

That hadn't come to be. It couldn't, needless to say:

177

nothing lasts. What remains in this instance are a few words and the photograph: "Thought you might want this." Unreasonably, that is precisely what I want, for even though I don't remember the event, I do indeed want to be five, I want my father to be there beside me, leaning against the wall, I want to squint into the sun and see my mother and the camera and hear the shutter click and have her walk towards us and my father take her place so she can sit beside me in her turn, or better still, ask some passing stranger to please take a picture of the three of us together and so freeze the moment and not let time move on and have us go, inevitably, each our separate way.

Just how that separation came about I am unable to say. For a long time I blamed my father. I blamed my mother. Later I blamed myself, mostly for shutting my father out, both shamefully and shamelessly, after the night I helped to carry him upstairs, making of that a divider that it may not have been. Confused, I stayed out much of the time, teaming up with an older boy from another school, to play football, the two of us, taking turns as goalkeeper, or spy on girls, or make our way onto forbidden building sites, where we would fantasize about running away with a travelling circus. When my father walked out, one month and three days before my twelfth birthday, I wasn't even home.

I take down the photo album from the bookcase, an unfinished project begun long ago, and open it, uncertain of how far I got – most of the pictures that haven't been thrown away or lost are in folders in my desk, along with strips of negatives. The album starts, I see, not the way I thought with studio shots of my parents, but with me as a baby – photos that I may have found interesting until age six or seven but probably not after that. Next comes my first birthday, followed by outdoor scenes interrupted by birthdays two, and three, and four: there I am, on my feet, standing or walking or sitting on a swing or in a sandpit, demolishing a sandcastle, built no doubt by someone else, with a small plastic spade, or tripping over a football, with a look of surprise. In the last picture, at the top of a page, I am in the garden of a house I recognize as ours, before we moved. There was, I know, a fence and a gate that I was not to open, leading onto a park or village green. If the pictures come in the right order, I would have been four at the time – the pictures of my fifth birthday, if there are any, must be in the desk.

A memory surfaces abruptly: I hear loud voices from a crowd of people in the park beyond the fence and close my eyes to try and recall the scene. This I can't do with any certainty. The people are excited. Are they laughing? They may be. I must have looked up at the kitchen window and, seeing no one there, squeezed through the gate, but this is no more than a guess. The crowd forms a dense wall. Suddenly a gap opens up and through the gap I see a man on the ground, screaming, staring at some ghastly sight above him, kicking his legs, flailing his arms. It is scary. The gap closes. I back away.

The incident is no less confusing now than it must have been as it occurred, which may be why it has stayed with me all these years, however incomplete, to reappear at a time when so much else is gone. "Just some drunk," I hear my mother say. "Let's see what's on TV" – or was that on a different occasion altogether? I couldn't say.

"Just some drunk." I close the album, snap it shut: it has a strap and a small buckle, as if to keep the photos safely locked away. Someday I must finish the project and add whatever pictures I would like to keep. I should at least move past my childhood, into my teens – my fatherless years. But that is not an accurate description of what followed: I am as fatherless today as I was then.

Still, nothing can change that. The note, the only one I have received in over thirty years, has it exactly right, except for the tense: "Thought you might want this." I put it back in the envelope in which it came. Too bad that it can't be.

About the author
Alongside a few poems and shorter pieces, stories by L F Roth have appeared on the web Segora (2012) as well as in anthologies brought out by Biscuit Publishing (2011), Earlyworks Press (2012, 2013, 2014) and Bridge House Publishing (2014).

Snowflakes and Good Deeds

T. D. Holland

In Sheffield we had proper winters, just like the ones you see on Christmas cards. Winter for us was one big snow covered world, and I am talking deep snow.

The negatives to this winter wonderland were, the difficulty getting out of the house in the first place. Our house on Cullabine Road seemed to be situated in a wind tunnel. You would know it had snowed because in the morning you would wake up to complete silence, as if the whole house was soundproofed.

One of the strange things about the snow was the fact it didn't make the house overly cold. Again it was as though the snow had cocooned us.

Mum would rush down stairs and quickly get the fire started and the kettle on. We would all scurry down stairs and be welcomed with a roaring fire and a warm cup of tea.

"By the way." Mum would say. "The door's blocked."

"Oh dear. Does that mean no school?" I would reply, a look of hope on my face.

Now our school was old and the pipes were on their last legs and these undependable beast would bust if snow fell too deep. This my dear friends was not a sad occasion for us, in fact it was a time of rejoicing as a snow day was a fun day.

"Nothing has been said on the radio yet, but there's still time." We would all sit expectantly by the radio, hoping our school would be read out on the list of schools closed that day.

Going back to the problem of the front door. Our

solution was to lower me out of the front window, with a small spade. No this wasn't child labour, this was fun.

I would get my jeans on and a big coat, grab my wellies and I was off, or should I say out of the window. The snow would be fresh and crisp and it would fall away from the door like sand. I would then bang my booted feet on the mat outside, shaking the snow off, then enter through snow cleared door and back for another warm drink.

"Bad news Tracey." Said Dad.

"No way, how can we go to school in this snow. There will be no heating and I will freeze to death." Then I would see dad smiling.

"Dad, you're evil and you will go to hell." I would tell him.

"Well at least it will be hot. And I will have Mum to keep me company. Won't I my darling wife?" Mum would reply by throwing a cushion at him.

"Ignore him Tracey. The radio has said your school is closed today."

Education is great and I am so pleased my parents fought to get us a great education. I love school, but who wouldn't love a snow day?

Even though it was still early, every kid would be awake, ready and out before nine. There is nothing like snow and a free day from school to bring every single one of them scurrying into their wellies and outside for a major snow ball fight before nine thirty.

We didn't need toys as such, as snowballs gave you everything for a good game. Some of us had sledges, nice plastic ones in bright colours. Lucky ones had the big wood ones their Dads had made, these were speed races that could carry three kids. We would zoom down our road, showing no fear. I cannot believe none of us got flattened by cars at the bottom. I think the cars went slower because they knew speedy youngsters would be about.

If you didn't have a sledge it didn't matter. The road would eventually become one big slide and you could start at the top of the road and skid all the way down to the bottom, well unless you miscalculated and ended up on your bum. You did not cry, we were tougher than that. No we just got back up, everyone laughing at our wet bums and we would carry on.

The cold never bothered us, we were so busy running around that we were like mini ovens and generated our own heat.

It was also funny to watch people trying to get to work. There was a bit of an odd tradition in Sheffield, well I think it was a tradition. I know we did it on the Manor, but maybe it was because we were a little unusual. People would open the door ready to go to work and on their feet they were wearing old woollen socks to stop them slipping.

We had to laugh as this would look so funny, watching these people of all ages desperately trying to stagger down the path. They couldn't go on the road as we had already iced it over with our skidding.

Most people didn't have a car and even if you had, there would be no way that you would be driving it anyway. The roads were so bad that the car would slip and slide and usually end up backed up on the kerb, or causey edge as we called it in Sheffield. The only way for people to get to work was by bus or by Shank's pony or in other words to walk.

The buses weren't too bad when we were little and seemed to be more mobile in bad weather than now. I also think we were tougher in those days and not afraid to walk to work, if necessary and if you were a little late, you didn't get any grief from your bosses.

We had a shop at the bottom of our road, called Alan Thorpe. He and his wife Elaine, always made sure the shop was open in this kind of weather and they sold things like milk and tea. This place was a life saver, as was the Co-op across the road.

In this kind of bad weather everyone stuck together, nobody was left without.

Even we kids did what we could; nobody moaned as we were taught to respect our elders. So when the snow began to fall and its white carpet began to settle, out came the troops, ready for day of good deeds.

My Dad wouldn't let us take money for certain things. If we did a favour for someone, you did it because you wanted to help, not because you wanted something back. He hated bad manners and always said older people deserve our respect.

So when it seemed as though it would be impossible for the old people on our street to get out of their houses, off we went to help.

At the bottom of our road and just around the corner were the Almhouses.

These were supposed to be charitable buildings. In these would live elderly people who were too old to work and didn't have enough to pay rent. Sometimes people who worked in the steel industry were allowed to live there. But as benefits were introduced any pensioner could live there. They were different from the other houses and had their own communal gardens and benches outside, so the name almhouses stuck.

When we used to go to school in the summer, many of the elderly people would be outside chatting with one another outside on the benches. As we passed Mum would always stop and chat, knowing all their names.

Back to the winter deeds.

"Is it still snowing bad outside?" Mum would ask.

"It's coming down fast mum and it's covering," I would reply.

"Go and see if anyone needs help at the Almhouses."

Mum would make sure that I was wrapped up warm and she gave me her trolley to put the groceries in. This was like a shopping bag on wheels and made it easier for me to carry more things and keep them dry. Mum would fret if I was carrying anything glass and fell and cut myself. So off I trotted with the blue striped trolley.

I would try to find some of my friends outside, or if there was nobody about I would call for them, then off we would go to see who needed what.

All of the old one knew us and were quick to take up the offer of help. I would take the shopping list of about three at a time, and they would put the money in an old purse mum gave me for the job. Then off I would go first heading down to the Co-op.

They knew me in there too.

"Morning Trace, you got some shopping lists from the Almhouses?"

"Yep." Then I would hand them the lists and the purse with the three pockets, this kept the money separate and the change they would get too.

People would ask for the basics like bread and milk. Or tins of meat, soup, and buns. But sometimes I would be asked for things like Steradent.

At first I would just take it like I was asked, but my curiosity got the better of me and I had to ask Dad.

"It's for our teeth." Dad laughed.

"Is it like toothpaste? Do you have to mush it up to put it on the toothbrush?" It seemed a very drawn out job and I couldn't see why they didn't just use normal toothpaste.

Dad asked Mum to show me her teeth. So Mum slipped them out. This always made me laugh. It was because Mum's teeth were false and when they were out of her mouth her whole face looked kind of rubbery and her mouth looked like a train tunnel.

Dad on the other hand wouldn't wear his teeth as he said it made him feel sick. This never hindered him and Mum said his gums were like steel, and that Dad could gum anything to death. I was used to seeing Dad's saggy face without his teeth and it was impossible to imagine what he would have looked like with them. They just sat in the cupboard in the bathroom and they would stare at you in the morning when you opened the cupboard to get your tooth brush and toothpaste.

"So what do they do with the Steradent Dad?"

"Well you take your teeth out at night and put them into a glass of water, then you pop a couple of these in and it cleans your teeth while you sleep."

I was amazed. What a neat thing. I could understand why it would be important not to run out of this miracle stuff.

I was also expected to go to and buy the old people cigarettes. There wasn't any real law prohibiting this when I was little. And you didn't have to buy a full packet neither.

"Can I have a packet of five for Mrs Skinner?" Sometimes I would even ask for three and the shop keeper would break open a packet and take the three cigarettes out.

I hated everything about cigarettes, the smell and the way it made the walls, doors and ceiling a horrid sticky yellow. It clung to everything and sometimes when I came home from school, you practically had to swim through the smoke to get to the living room.

Mum and Dad both smoked constantly. I think this is why all the three of their kids had chest problems. My brother had bronchitis, I had bad croup that made me sound like a very angry dog. Janet got the worst as she had the two holes in her heart. We had seen how this had affected not only us, but mum and dad and because of that none of us kids ever smoked.

It was the normal thing to do, and that's why I was walking in the snow to collect them as some of the olds ones would rather starve than go without that lifesaving drag of a cigarette.

I wasn't allowed to take money for the errands I ran. The old ones knew this and in their wisdom found a way around this.

I would come home with cakes and sweets, all of which Dad didn't mind me accepting. I know this made the old people feel ok too.

I never minded doing this as I loved to feel useful. Dad knew this and I think it made him prouder. Even now if I see someone in need I try to do what I can. For this I am very grateful for the morals my parents instilled in me, for helping time to become the best person I can.

About the author

Tracey has been writing all her life and has just graduated from Nottingham University with a BA in Professional and Creative Writing.

Her main interests are Memoirs and Children's writing and she has finished her first novel, a Memoir titled, *Born In The Change*.

In 2015 her Novel was long listed in the Mslexia memoir competition.

She is now looking to get an agent and publish her first novel.

Heart to Heart

Glynis Scrivens

Brenda glanced nervously at her watch. Three o'clock. Her daughter Alice would be here any moment. She hadn't seen her for nearly twelve months. Was it really that long ago that Alice had stormed off, to live with her aunt in Surrey? Originally it was to be for a week, but her aunt had needed a hip replacement and Alice had offered to stay and help. Then she'd found a job locally.

The odd postcard had arrived, with snippets of news, and they'd exchanged birthday presents, but Brenda hadn't really felt they'd communicated. Not until last night's phone call when Alice had said she was driving up to see her. There'd been a wariness and tension in Alice's voice when she'd phoned her, but something else as well.

Was it possible after all this time that Alice too was hoping to find a bridge to link their troubled hearts?

She looked at the quilted wall hanging, which she'd made in the weeks after Alice had moved out. When her own heart had ached and swelled with grief.

A car pulled up outside. Brenda wiped the palms of her hands onto her jeans.

The first thing she noticed about Alice as she walked up the driveway was her hair. It was blonde, just as it had been when she was young. She stood by the window to watch the sunlight glinting off her daughter's hair.

Somehow she'd never got used to seeing Alice with black hair. Never understood the need to cover up who she was.

Alice had always covered things up. That'd been the problem.

And Brenda had never really felt able to deal with the sorry situations that'd resulted.

Maybe the blonde hair was a reflection of other changes? A small ray of hope entered her heart.

The doorbell rang, and Brenda hurried down the hall.

She clasped Alice in her arms. "I love your hair," she managed.

Alice shrugged. "I wanted a change." Her voice was subdued.

Brenda led her into the kitchen. She knew Alice hated any kind of fuss, so she started to make coffee. She'd let her daughter do the talking. It'd be silly to get the visit off on the wrong footing after all this time. She'd never quite known what to say to her, even now.

Alice sat down at the wooden table and looked around.

Brenda carefully measured the coffee beans into her old-fashioned grinder. It looked as though it belonged in another century. To a time when people weren't always in a hurry. When there was time for families to sit around the kitchen table and sort out their differences. When people spent more time simply talking to each other. And listening. That's why she'd bought it, when she'd seen it in the charity shop. To remind herself to walk through time, not run.

There'd been plenty of time to think once Alice had moved out. She wanted to learn from the mistakes she'd made.

Soon the air was rich with the fresh intoxicating aroma.

"What's your news?" Brenda reached into the cupboard for cups and saucers. Another old-fashioned choice. Everyone else seemed to use mugs for their coffee now. But these cups were a rich buttercup, with bright daisies. Too cheerful to resist. And big enough for a decent-sized coffee.

"I'll wait till you're sitting down."

Brenda's heart hovered slowly in mid-air. She felt the heat rising from her chest and suffusing her face. She'd noticed Alice's complexion was pale and there were dark circles under her eyes. She daren't think what it might mean.

"Don't look like that, Mum," Alice said. "It's nothing bad. I just don't want to shock you."

"My heart can't take much." Brenda sat down at the table, beside her daughter.

"Your heart's pretty tough," Alice said. "It's needed to be, hasn't it?"

Words didn't come. All Brenda could do was nod. Why had Alice come today? What was she trying to tell her?

She didn't have to wait. The words tumbled out.

Alice reached across and held her hand. "I'm going to have a baby."

The tears fell of their own accord, as Brenda's arms wrapped her daughter close in an awkward embrace.

"I didn't even know you were in a relationship. Who is the father?" More questions flooded her mind, before Alice could begin to answer. "How will you be able to support a baby? Are you still living in Surrey?"

"His name is Max and he's a high school teacher. I want you to meet him."

Brenda sipped her coffee thoughtfully. "Maybe I could drive down to Surrey for a few days?"

Alice's eyes sparkled. "We're decided to move back here. Max's got a transfer to my old high school." She paused. "I know it's a lot to grasp but I'm hoping you'll be okay with it all."

Brenda gave a deep sigh and felt her shoulders relax.

"You had me worried when you said I'd need to be sitting down. I thought you'd lost your job, or decided to live the other side of the world."

"I'm moving, but it's to be closer to home, not further away. I don't know anything about babies. And neither does Max."

The word 'home' lingered in Brenda's mind. "Just learn to trust your instincts. That's what worked for me." She paused, "And I learnt to listen to my own mother."

Alice pouted, as if to protest, but her lips twitched into a smile. The smile grew, till the tongue stud appeared.

They were both conscious of it.

"I put you through a lot, didn't I?" Alice was suddenly serious again.

Brenda looked for words to explain the gulf between her expectations and the angry young life she'd produced. "It wasn't easy. I had to do a lot of soul-searching. We're such different people."

Alice held her hand tightly. "Thanks for never giving up on me."

"I think I should say the same to you. We've both had to learn a lot, haven't we?"

Alice's eyes suddenly lit up. "That's one of the reasons I came today," she said. "I want to learn how to sew."

Brenda wiped her eyes. "I've waited years to hear you say that." She bit her tongue. "That sounds all wrong, doesn't it? I don't mean I expected you to be like me. It's just that I've wanted something to share with you and with all your artistic talent, sewing seemed something we could have in common."

"I was too stubborn to see that," Alice said. "I always felt you wanted a clone and that I didn't fit the bill."

"That's my fault. I was so worried about your father's health that I couldn't see the impact it was all having on you."

"Let's not talk about fault. We all made mistakes. I've gone through it all with Max and he's helped me realize that."

"Your Max sounds as though he's good for you."

Alice's eyes glistened. "He's helped me turn my life around."

"How did you two find each other?"

"I've been working part time in the admin section at the same school where Max teaches," Alice said. "Once we got talking, he suggested I study art in the evenings so I could find work that's more suited to my talents."

"How does he feel about the baby?" Brenda couldn't help asking.

"It's come as a huge surprise to us both, but he's very practical." Alice smiled. "And he's excited. He wants to be a hands-on dad."

"What about your art?"

"Max suggested we both work part-time once the baby's old enough." She held Brenda's hand. "There's something else I want to tell you, and I hope it doesn't upset you. If the baby's a boy, we'd like to name him after Dad."

Brenda wiped her eyes, but there was a smile on her face. "When's your baby due?"

"I've only just found out that I'm two months pregnant."

"That gives us lots of time for you to learn how to sew."

"I really want to be able to sew clothes for my baby. Learn to mend. All that stuff."

"We can start on the basics today, if you've got time."

Alice looked at the quilted wall hanging, behind Brenda. "Do you think I'll ever be able to make a quilt like that?"

Brenda bit the inside of her bottom lip. *I hope you never need to*, she thought. Perhaps she should have put it away this morning?

The quilt had evolved from a period of intense heartache and despair. A time when Brenda had felt there was no one she could turn to for solace. Somehow she'd simply needed to work things out in this way. It was her life depicted on this quilt, in a form she could understand. By hanging it on the wall in the living room, it reminded her that anything could be dealt with. Its presence reassured her, whenever life threw something seemingly impossible in her path.

She looked at the quilt, touching the line of black embroidery that stretched across the width.

"This stitch is easy to learn," she said. "It's a bit like blanket stitch."

Alice drew her arm through Brenda's.

"Is that an old-fashioned clothes line?" she asked. "Why are there hearts on it?"

Brenda shook her head and felt her eyes moistening. "It's barbed wire," she said softly. "Our hearts were all on barbed wire. And they were hurting. That's what I wanted to show."

Brenda felt Alice's arm tighten around her, before being released.

She watched as her daughter rolled up the sleeves of her cardigan.

They both looked at her forearms. Over the years the crisscross scars had faded to a soft pearl. But in Brenda's memory they were still raw and angry, as the day she'd first seen them.

"My life felt like barbed wire too," Alice said. "I think I must've been suffering from depression to do this to myself."

"That's what I worried about. And you seemed to blame yourself for your father's heart attack."

Alice nodded. "When I came home from work and saw an ambulance parked outside, I freaked out. I'd argued with him that morning."

"We should've told you earlier about his heart condition but we didn't want to worry you."

They both looked quietly at the quilt.

"Why did you make your heart different to everyone else's?" Alice asked.

Brenda looked at the four hearts sitting on a line of barbed wire. With a trail of tiny hearts raining down from one of the hearts. That heart was Brenda's.

"My heart broke when I found out that you'd cut yourself. I felt very alone. These tiny hearts are meant to symbolize what was going on inside me."

Alice brushed her eyes. "It was me that I hated, never you. I blamed myself for his death."

"I felt that, but my heart kept leaking tears, I didn't seem to have any control over it." She paused. "I was so overwhelmed by my own emotions that I didn't really grasp what you must've been going through."

"I wasn't exactly approachable."

"No, but if I had my time over again I'd try harder to find help for you."

"Don't beat yourself up about it, Mum. I don't think I'd have opened up to anyone back then."

Alice gently traced the bright cherry-coloured outline of Brenda's heart with her forefinger.

The tenderness in the gesture brought fresh tears to Brenda's eyes. She tried to will them away, as she watched her daughter.

The years peeled away. She remembered sitting here at the dining room table, a piece of soft red cloth in front of her. On the table were hearts in all shapes and sizes. Choosing which heart would represent each of them had been the hardest part. She'd wept silently for the loss of innocence. For the hurt. For the disillusion.

She'd found a sturdy-looking heart for Daniel, to reflect his strength of character. Her son's was solid too, but slighter. He'd grow into the sturdiness over time. It was already in his eyes.

She'd noticed one of the pieces had fallen onto the floor. When she picked it up, the fabric had crush marks. She'd tried to smooth them out with her hand, but they'd resisted. *This one is Alice's*, she'd thought. She knew she should iron it but couldn't bring herself to do it. Solutions couldn't be forced on Alice's heart. She'd have to find a gentler way. And there'd been one. She'd carefully rubbed it and stretched it around her hot tea cup. That had smoothed out the worst of the crush marks.

Love always found a way, she reflected, as she watched her daughter now.

Alice was still looking intently at the row of hearts, sitting on the barbed wire.

"I've only just noticed something," she said. "Why is your heart a bit bigger than the others?"

Brenda had instinctively chosen this heart to reflect her own that sad afternoon. It'd only been later that she too had noticed that it was slightly more substantial than the others. She was glad that Alice was looking at the quilt closely enough to see this subtlety. But she felt self-conscious too. Her heart was no bigger or better than anyone else's. It'd simply felt swollen at the time. Now she saw it differently. Perhaps all mothers needed to develop more heart, as they learnt to grow into the role?

"Your heart will grow too, as you help your baby through life," she said. "Just enjoy every moment with your baby. Those early years seem to pass very quickly."

"Did you enjoy your moments with me? Despite everything?"

Brenda took her into her arms, this slight girl who would soon become a mother herself. Alice's blonde head sank into her shoulder, leaving a sweet scent of fresh shampoo. She held tightly to Brenda in a way that was breath-taking. Opening so many doors that'd been closed and locked in recent years. It was a warm heartfelt hug, one she'd waited years to receive.

And for the first time she realized that true healing had taken place, transforming the angry wounds into pearly scars. On Alice's arms. And also on her own heart.

"We had good times," Brenda answered. "Remember our beach holidays? We all seemed to relax as soon as we saw the ocean."

"Maybe we should've lived by the sea?" Alice said. "It might've suited us better."

"Too late now for what ifs. We've got a whole new future opening up."

She thought back over the years.

There'd been good moments when she'd felt she didn't deserve so much happiness. And there'd been terrible times when she'd felt crushed and completely inadequate. And now a new baby was coming into their lives, another heart that would need to be looked after and nurtured. This time by her daughter.

Brenda realized that it was time she made another quilt.

She would need to find a new way of expressing this

insight. Of showing how pearls of wisdom came into being.

Perhaps she'd use oyster shells this time? They could be nestled in a bed of sand, in the warm nurturing waters of the ocean.

She could throw away the black cotton, and buy some gold silk.

About the author

Glynis Scrivens writes short stories, and has been published in Australia, UK, Ireland, South Africa, US and Scandinavia. She writes for *Writers' Forum* (UK), and has had articles in *The New Writer, Pets, Steam Railway, Ireland's Own,* and *Writing* magazine. Her work has appeared in seven anthologies. She lives in Brisbane with her family and a menagerie of hens, ducks, dogs, lorikeets, and a cat called Myrtle. Her first book *Edit is a Four-Letter Word* was published by John Hunt in 2015.

Her website is at www.glynisscrivens.com/wp.

What's In a Name?

Vanessa Horn

It was very sudden, I'll grant you that; one moment I was staring out of the office window, calculating how many more minutes until I could nip out for my ciggie break and the next... well, to put it bluntly, I was dying! Truthfully, when the mist had swirled around me, I'd thought – as would be perfectly natural on a Friday morning – I was just daydreaming. Albeit realistically. After all, I wasn't expecting this; I wasn't ill, involved in an accident or even that old! Anyhow, this pastel haze was quickly followed by short cinematic-type excerpts. Of my life. The good bits, the bad bits, even the mediocre bits. By then, of course, I knew I was in trouble – we've all heard all about those moments just before death, when your life is projected before you. In order for you to take stock, I suppose. So now it was just a question of waiting for the bright light and guardian angel to appear and that was me. Done.

Not that I wasn't annoyed about this occurrence. If I'd had time to gather my thoughts rationally, I'd definitely have been peeved that I was dying way before I was ready (although I suppose most people *would* say that). But equally, I'd have berated myself at my lack of achievement in life; the things I hadn't done, hadn't said, hadn't realised. The usual really. But, as I said before, it was all happening so fast. Too fast.

And before I could even protest, there he was – my guardian angel! Or so I assumed, he being the only person travelling towards me on a strong beam of radiance with his arms outstretched. Wide smile on his face. Although he was rather shabbily clothed, to be truthful – not quite what you'd expect. Man at Oxfam I'd have described him, if pushed to do so. Still, it didn't do to be too picky about these things; I myself was not the sharpest dresser in my work or social circle. Good clothes didn't necessarily maketh the man, after all.

Before I could so much as pose a question, or even comment on this turn of events, the slightly dishevelled – angel? – grabbed my hand and quickly led me into the beam of light. Whereupon we were whizzed upwards. And innerwards too, if that makes sense. Next thing I knew, we were standing outside an impressive pair of golden gates surrounded by whirling clouds and mists of sorbet-delicious colours. In front of this entrance was an elderly man, sporting a long beard and carrying a bejewelled clipboard. All rather clichéd, I felt at this point. And still incredibly dream-like; I wouldn't have been surprised if I'd blinked and suddenly found myself back at the office, still staring out of the window. But I didn't. Couldn't.

The older man peered at me curiously, from head to toe. Then slowly shook his head. Frowning deeply, he turned to address my scruffy companion, his voice low and resonating. "He's not expected."

Now I was the one to frown (though probably not so impressively). I turned to my scruffy companion – now to be referred to as SC. My voice came out shakily and at least a semitone higher than normal. "What does he mean, *not expected?*"

At this point, SC was shifting nervously from foot to foot, turning an unfetching shade of pale pink. Ignoring me, he spoke to the other man first. "But I went to the correct place, sir, followed all the rules like you're supposed to – he *is* the right one: Drake Barton!"

The older man let out an elongated groan, slapping the side of his head noisily with his palm. "No! You fool, you were supposed to fetch Blake Downton! *Blake Downton!*"

SC blinked and then shuddered, seeming to physically shrink by the second while we stared at him accusingly. Muttering something that sounded a little like "Bloody dyslexia!" he turned away from us, giving one of the golden gates a hefty kick. I'm assuming it was pretty solid, for all the impact he made on it. After yelling and hopping around in pain for a few moments, he finally collapsed onto the ground in an untidy heap.

Shaking my head in bewilderment, I addressed the elderly man. "So it's a mistake, then? I wasn't supposed to die today? I can go back?"

He looked downwards. Sighed, rather protractedly, it seemed. His voice was considerably softer now. "Yes, yes and, regrettably… *no.*"

I processed this information relatively quickly. For me, anyhow. "No I can't go back? Why not, if I shouldn't have been brought here in the first place?"

Now he looked up, his eyes meeting mine. Eyes of deep brown, tinged with rings of black. I thought I could detect some sympathy in his expression. "I'm afraid once you've travelled through, the way back is sealed. For ever. You will just have to wait now until it's your time to enter."

Could this really be correct? "But when *is* my time to enter?" I was feeling more than a little anxious now, to be perfectly truthful. I've never been renowned for my patience, and there didn't seem to be a lot of action here. If I had to stay around for too long, I was in danger of becoming incredibly bored.

The elderly man (EM) consulted his clipboard list. Turned over a page. And another. Finally, after what seemed like an eternity of rustling sheets, he sighed then mumbled his reply: "September 2nd 2035."

"What? *What?* I'm not hanging around for" – I made a rapid calculation – "over twenty years!" I threw another accusing scowl at SC who was now resting against the gates, carefully inspecting his injured toes.

Reddening once again, he muttered, "Sorry," and then, seemingly devoid of any verbal expansion, returned his gaze to his foot.

I rolled my eyes Heavenwards – obviously now closer than it had been this time yesterday, albeit still inaccessible – and addressed EM again. "What do you suggest you do while I wait?" I was trying to stay polite; nevertheless, I could hear a querulousness in my voice. However, surely that was understandable in the circumstances?

EM considered this. Scratched his beard thoughtfully. "Legislation states – not that this type of misfortune occurs very often, of course – that you are not permitted to 'hang around', as you put it. Not by yourself, anyway. Therefore, you will need supervising until such time as you can legally enter Heaven. Given that it was one individual – and one individual only – that put you in this unfortunate position, it would seem reasonable that he should be your appointed custodian during this time."

SC and I exchanged dubious glances; neither of us looked exactly thrilled at the idea.

Disregarding the hostile vibes, EM walked over to SC. Tugged him ungently to his feet and spoke firmly. "If you carry out this mission successfully then you *may* be able to continue in your position of Retriever. Eventually. Providing you also undertake some additional training for your reading problems, of course!"

SC sighed, seemingly unimpressed. Exhaled deeply. Ultimately, possibly having weighed up his options and finding them limited, he shrugged and turned to me. Clapped a hand on my shoulder and led me away from EM and the golden gates. "Come on then."

As we strolled away, through the mists of colours and haze, I glanced at my newly-appointed guardian. He hadn't uttered a word since our departure from the golden gates, and was seemingly deep in thought. I cleared my throat noisily. "So, what now? Where are we supposed to go for two decades?"

Suddenly grinning, SC drew me closer. "Right. Now, don't get too excited, but I think I know of someone who can help get you into Heaven before your time."

I looked at him dubiously. Far from being excited, I couldn't help wondering if this was going to be yet another mess-up.

y reserve must have been obvious, for SC puffed out his cheeks indignantly, frowning. "Look, it's got nothing to do with reading, ok?"

I considered. Nodded slowly – what did I have to lose? "Alright, let's do it."

There was something about this strange place that made it impossible to identify how much time had passed; it could've been minutes or even hours since we had set off, but at some point we reached a clearing in the vapours. SC brought us to a halt. "Here."

I looked around curiously, but before I had time to comment, I spotted a dark shape looming out of the mist. "The Accelerator," SC whispered.

A large figure stood before us. Raised a wiry eyebrow. "Yes?" His voice was unsurprisingly deep, matching his physique and demeanour perfectly.

SC quickly outlined our predicament, predictably

glossing over his own failings in the erroneous scenario. He wittered on for some time before concluding breathlessly, "So we need to get Blake – um, Drake – into Heaven as soon as possible."

The Accelerator was silent for a few moments whilst studying us both. Then he replied. "And if I were to… *help* you with this dilemma, what would you be able to offer me in return?"

SC paused, then shrugged wordlessly, holding out his hands. Empty. Without a lot of optimism, I quickly delved into my trouser pockets: a packet of chewing gum, 97p and – unexpectedly – a small ball bearing. Being whisked away without time to throw my jacket on was obviously not to my advantage.

I thought quickly. Blurted out, "Maybe there's something I can do for you – a favour of some sort?"

His voice seemed gruffer now. "A *favour?*"

"Yes – anything!" I cringed; I'm not usually one to beg, but, then again, have never been found in this type of situation. Desperate measures and all that…

The Accelerator considered my plea, looking me up and down as if to determine what use I could possibly be. Eventually, an idea seemed to occur to him. He pursed his lips in – I hoped – an approximation of a smile. "Well… I suppose as you are relatively fresh, it *would* mean you have an advantage; you'd be able to access certain areas that I cannot. Areas such as the Edge…"

There was a sudden gasp from SC, indicating that this errand was evidently not going to be an agreeable one. But I remained silent, waiting for the Accelerator to continue. Wanted to find out more before I made my decision.

Possibly encouraged by a lack of immediate refusal, the Accelerator moved closer, now even taking one of my hands in his. "The Edge is the hairline precipice between life and death. Although you can't step back to Earth, from there you gain a view of the goings-on – can observe friends, relatives back on Earth. I – I need to find out how my family are coping without me, two years on… If you could just get close enough to see that they are in good form, it would bring me considerable peace of mind."

I thought about his request. "If I travelled to this *Edge* – is it dangerous?" As soon as I'd said the words, I couldn't help feeling a bit foolish; after all, I was *dead* – what worse fate could befall me, after all?

The Accelerator bit his lip. Heaved a sigh. "There is a *slight* risk of being lost between the two civilisations, but that's only if you go too close to Earth; with vigilance, you'll have no problem. At all. However, if you don't take care, well…"

Beside me, SC shuddered, whispering, "You don't want to know!"

And actually I didn't. I already knew that I was going to undertake this mission, dangerous or not. For, basically, there was no way I was going to wander around in the mists for twenty years, waiting for my legal entrance to Heaven. I nodded at the Accelerator. "I'll do it."

Truthfully, as I proceeded to follow the swirling path that I'd swiftly been pointed at, I felt no nerves, no fears. Rather, I was more gratified that, finally, I had something purposeful to do. Something constructive. I could do this – I had to. I increased my pace, ignoring SC dragging his heels in my wake. Eventually, I was aware of him sitting down behind me with a noisy grunt. "This is as far as I can go," he said, with obvious relief. "I'll wait for you here."

I continued on my way, observing that the coloured

haze around me was now thickening and making it difficult to see very far ahead. Now, for the first time since leaving the Accelerator, I experienced a slight unease; how would I know when I reached the Edge – would it be obvious where to stop or would I accidentally blunder on and fall over the precipice? And even if I didn't, would I be able to recognise the Accelerator's family in order to report back to him successfully? So many doubts. But, despite my anxieties, I kept walking. What else could I do?

Eventually, I spotted a thin contour of land in front. Was that it? Had I reached the Edge? My heart fluttered; could I really be so close to Earth; to my former life? I hurried towards the solid-seeming strip, all the while keeping aware of my footfalls, anxious not to cross the invisible but lethal line which would render me misplaced. As I grew closer, I slowed down – took even more care. And yes, I could now see how thin the Edge actually was; one step too far and you *would* be lost. I stopped still and peered down at the void which separated the two civilisations; I could see nothing but blackness down there, although – when I listened carefully – I was aware of a faint howling sound. Lost souls? Demons? I didn't care to find out – I needed to get on with my mission and achieve my goal.

Averting my eyes from the deep chasm, I gazed instead across at Earth. Although it was recognisable *as* Earth, I didn't perceive it in the same way as when I'd existed there. For a start, as my eyes travelled across the land, it seemed, initially, just as a whirling juxtaposition of free-frame scenarios. Then, when I concentrated on any particular region, the people and objects in that zone would immediately become animated, seemingly going about their daily lives. I could even make out features, expressions. Hear their comments, observations. Incredible! I zoomed in and out for a while, deliberately resisting the temptation to locate my own family; I really didn't think I was ready to witness their reactions to my departure. I then realised that what I need to do was to scan along systematically until I located the Accelerator's brethren – whoever and wherever they might be – then focus in. Obtain the details and particulars that the Accelerator was so anxious to find out about. Right...

As I've mentioned before, time travels differently here. Certainly not in minutes and hours, as far as I can tell. So I only know that after a specific time period, my eyes began to feel tired with straining, my soul dispirited with disappointment. After all, I didn't really know who I was looking for – how could I possibly know when I found them?

Suddenly, my fevered concentration was startled by a noise behind. Quickly turning round, I was surprised to see SC nervously approaching me. Unexpectedly pleased to see him, I was nevertheless uneasy that he had come this far. "I thought you couldn't—"

He nodded quickly, his eyes flicking nervously towards the Edge. "I know – it's highly irregular, not to mention dangerous – but I felt guilty about letting you go alone; it's my fault you're in this predicament, after all. My conscience told me I had to come and help!"

I glanced at his face; he was sweating profusely but seemed to have a previously unseen determination. I was quite impressed, despite my previous lack of faith in him. "Thanks... but just be careful you don't get too close. Have you any idea what I'm looking for here?"

He nodded again, his eyes peering anxiously over the edge of the precipice. "Yes, that's why I came; I was with the team who collected the Accelerator – not that he was called that then – and I've seen his family, have an idea where they can be located." He saw me glance at him knowingly. He blushed a little. "And before you say anything, no I didn't get that one wrong."

I raised my eyebrows resignedly. Just me then. Well, I supposed it didn't matter that much now – it was too late to change things *and* we had a job to accomplish. "Ok, let's get this done then."

SC proved invaluable, obviously. I don't know how long I'd have had to stay at the Edge, scanning frantically until I got some kind of clue as to who I was looking for, but with him there, at least I had some kind of an advantage. And, as if to prove my point, pretty soon he gave a small exclamation. Pointed downwards. "There – that's them!"

I stared curiously in the direction of his finger. Yes, I couldn't mistake the dark swarthiness that marked this family out as belonging to the Accelerator. A middle-aged woman, two adult sons… ok, well, they looked happy enough. Healthy. Going about their daily lives. But… who was this with them – this tall blond man? I frowned, wondering if he was another member of the family. A distant cousin, maybe? SC and I exchanged glances. He shrugged but indicated that we should tune in – gain more information. As we listened and watched, it became apparent that the Accelerator's wife had done more than just survive since her husband had died; she'd obviously set up a new life for herself with a new man! Okaay…

Simultaneously, SC and I averted our eyes away from the family. Moved back from the Edge and sat a safe distance away. We contemplated silently then, finally, spoke at the same time:

"Do you think I should –?"

"What will you –?"

Our combined exclamations broke the uneasy atmosphere. Echoed all around the dispiriting place which was the Edge, and drifted way up high into the surrounding coloured mist. Eased the apprehension a little.

SC shot me a quick glance. "I'd heard the Accelerator was quite a villain in his time, you know. A good family man, yes, but underhand in his business dealings. Apparently."

I didn't find that hard to believe. "Mmm. I suppose the very fact that, even up here, he's running an underhand service doesn't commend him highly. Still…" Being a good family man *was* a strong redeeming feature. But was it enough? And, of course, the truth was that I needed him, flaws or not. So I had to make a decision.

SC was watching me anxiously. "I think we should to go back." He was obviously keen to return to the comparative safety of the mists.

I chewed my lip thoughtfully. "Yeah, we've seen all that's necessary. Now."

As we strolled back through the haze, my mind was whirling as much as the mists around us. I was thinking about what we'd witnessed. Mulling over my predicament. Thinking about life. Death. Compromises. I still had no idea exactly what I would tell the Accelerator but could only hope that the solution would come to me. Eventually.

The density lessening the further we walked, I gradually became more aware of my surroundings. Either I was becoming used to being here, or the whole experience was sharpening my senses. Now I could see the vapours not just as a swirling mass but rather as separate patterns, meanderings, configurations. I wondered if each one had a symbolism of a sort. Or perhaps they were forms of landmarks, directing individuals like a 3D map. Not that we had seen any person, either journeying to or from the Edge. But perhaps that was because of the risky nature of the area. I realised that we were lucky not to have any calamity happen to us while we were there.

Soon, from a distance up high, and seemingly deceptively small because of this, I could see the Accelerator watching our return. He strode swiftly towards us, his expression anxious. Apprehensive. *A family man.* Suddenly, my doubts dispersed. Taking a deep breath, I began to speak. Decisively. Assuredly. "I saw them. All is well – you have nothing to worry about." Slowly, his expression relaxed, forming a broad smile of thanks. He quickly raised a hand and directed a bright ray of light towards me, indicating that I was to come forward. Squinting, I could just about make out a small silver gate at the end of this beam. Unguarded. The back gate? Yes, it had to be. Right.

I levelled a quick glance at SC. He winked back at me, giving the thumbs up sign. Then turned round to leave, clicking his heels in the air in a celebratory manner. Laughing, I began to walk confidently into the radiance. I was ready to begin my new life.

About the author

Vanessa Horn is a Junior School teacher who first became interested in writing in 2012, when she took a sabbatical year off from work. Since then, she has written several hundred stories, some of which have been published in magazines, and others having won prizes in competitions. In July, a collection of twenty-two of her short stories – *Eclectic Moments* – was published by Alfie Dog Fiction.

Last Call for Air

Mike Scott Thomson

Jannik awoke early on the Monday morning, levered himself out of bed, and pulled up the blinds. A brighter, lighter air than usual flooded into the room. Overnight, the Hovedstaden had been liberally coated with a luminescent white, two or three inches thick: dappled and jagged in places, rounded and smooth in others. The Greenlanders would have a word for it, if Søndergaard was to be believed.

Jannik felt a sudden rush of hope. Just for once this development may put him on the right side of 'maybe'. He reached for his phone and opened the arrivals/departures app. A couple of swipes later he found what he was looking for: Copenhagen to Nuuk via Kangerlussuaq.

No delays. No cancellations. All flights, bang on time.

The news couldn't have been any worse.

The terminal was all glass and glare. The low winter sun fractured its way through the building, splaying translucent shadows across the airport's drop-off area. From the back seat of the taxi, Jannik turned his head and looked up, his eyes a quick glance up and down but the rest him unmoving. Not for the first time he recalled an expression he'd once learned in English – to 'fall' into a job – and wondered whether he could apply this maxim to himself, when he spent so much time in the air.

A year ago, it had been obvious upon his arrival at Kjær-Iversen that his role was mostly undefined. Ostensibly, 'Information Technology' was his department, *informationsteknologi*, but the *informations* involved in his day-to-day work had no appeal to him – beta-testing

210

programs, handling decimals and percentages, tax bands for different territories – and the *teknologi* side of the role was, for Jannik, merely fixing the numerous problems arising on a daily basis – logins, passwords, systems crashes. Such fails were almost always down to human error. His job, as it became apparent, was to clear up other people's mistakes.

With his Master's in Computer Science freshly imprinted on his CV, he knew he should achieve better. He could write programs able to process the same data in half the time, and, he estimated, at a quarter of the expense. But as a junior member of staff, straight out of university, he needed to be patient.

With the possible exception of his immediate manager, Birgita, everyone seemed to have a different idea about what he actually did. Even Søndergaard thought, as was evident during the flight back from the Nuuk conference last February, that his young new recruit's remit was a blurred hybrid of Customer Service and web design.

"Those are elements, yes…" were the only words Jannik managed to get in edgeways.

Søndergaard squatted down in the aisle, made an overly deliberate point of making eye contact, and leaned in conspiratorially. "Did you know," he said, "that the Eskimos have over a hundred words for snow?"

This was a complete change in subject from what had been little more than smalltalk, and Jannik had a sinking feeling that he was about to hear 'that speech'. As it happened Jannik did know about the Inuit and their supposed lexicon, but only because Søndergaard had said the very same thing at a training seminar six weeks before. Although Jannik could have sworn the number of words for snow back then had been fifty, not a hundred.

"No, I didn't," said Jannik. "That's fascinating…"

"And we design and sell," continued Søndergaard, "the best systems in the world. But you know that already, yes?"

Jannik nodded.

"And not only that, we have the best employees in the world," said Søndergaard, sweeping his hand down the aisle of the plane to the dozen delegates who had made the trip. "You could even say," he leaned even closer, so near that Jannik smelt brandy on the old CEO's breath, "we're so good, we can sell snow to the Eskimos."

Jannik had indeed heard all this before, but it still wasn't making much sense. Søndergaard was undoubtedly a sharp and savvy CEO, with business and management strengths too numerous to list – but effective use of metaphor was not one of them.

Søndergaard paused, as if he'd read his mind. "What I mean, is…" He squinted in concentration, as if trying to find the right term, then winced as he straightened his legs, rising to his feet. "If we are in the business of selling snow, we have to *understand* snow. And to *understand* snow, we need to *think* like snow."

Søndergaard should lay off the booze, thought Jannik.

"But," continued the CEO, "there's so much more to 'snow' than simply 'snow', yes?"

"Yes," Jannik said.

"I'm glad you agree," said Søndergaard. Having accomplished his mission seemingly to spare at least five minutes for a one-to-one with each of his employees, he turned back to Business Class, straightening the jacket on his designer suit. "New blood, new blood, very good." He headed back to his seat.

At thirty thousand feet above the Greenlandic ice

sheet, and only two months into his new job, Jannik leaned back, closed his eyes, and hoped all he needed to do was give it time.

Jannik disembarked the taxi, paid the driver and headed inside the terminal. He felt his inside jacket pocket for his passport and tickets. Still there. More's the pity, he thought.

In little over a year this was Jannik's fourth visit to Nuuk. The three previous journeys had yielded nothing extraordinary, hardly worth the large expense; a visit to the data centre on the outside of the small city (a soulless warehouse amidst rocks and bracken, installed there to take advantage of the cold climate), and, more often than not, a mid-Atlantic briefing and coding session with their American clients. Halfway between the two, and with most of their servers whirring contentedly in subzero temperatures, Greenland was the obvious choice.

In the past, Søndergaard had insisted on leading the European delegation. Birgita had usually come along too, and at least eight others from IT and procurement. Previously, Jannik's role was to set up the network and nip any technical problems in the bud. Yet this particular occasion was a new one. Sure, on the agenda was a customary visit to the data centre, which Jannik knew he could undertake without any trouble. However, afterwards, there was to be a meet up with representatives of a previously unheard-of company called Synatech which he was expected to attend on his own. Without Søndergaard. Without Birgita. Without anybody else from their branch at all.

At first, Jannik didn't understand. Was this his big chance? An opportunity to take that step up he so sorely wanted? At the moment he was little more than a junior troubleshooter. So what, precisely, was required of him?

213

Søndergaard had been typically vague. He'd simply said, in passing, "It'll do you good. Great experience. We have faith in you."

It was left to Birgita to set the record straight and give him more precise instructions.

"Synatech are the outsourcers," she told him.

"Who?" Jannik asked.

"Søndergaard wants them to take on Customer Services," she said. "He thinks they'll save us millions."

Jannik frowned. "Does our Customer Services team know this?"

"Not yet," said Birgita. "So it's, you know. Hush hush."

As Jannik walked to Air Greenland's check-in desk he thought of the team of a dozen people, all of whom would lose their jobs if this outsourcing went ahead. He knew them; he liked them. They were good, hardworking people. But presumably they were one type of 'snow' Søndergaard had no time for. So much for 'the best employees in the world'.

He greeted the girl at the desk. "The snow didn't stop you, then?"

"This time, no," she smiled. "We are not *Immaqa Air* today!"

Immaqa Air. What the Greenlanders affectionately, or perhaps resignedly, called their national airline: *Maybe Air*. A service at the mercy of the changeable, inclement weather; the same climate which, in a twist of circumstance, Kjær-Iversen made full use of.

"Have a nice flight," said the check-in girl, handing him back his papers.

The flights took most of the day. Jannik settled into a window seat by an emergency exit, stretched out his legs, and opened his laptop. The lines of coding appeared to dance and shuffle in kaleidoscopic patterns on the screen, no two symbols or digits staying still. Perhaps it was fatigue; his fault for delaying finishing the all-important beta-check until the last minute, when he'd had a whole month to prepare. But he didn't blame himself for leaving it for so long. He rubbed his eyes and clicked his laptop shut.

Outside, thousands of feet in the air, a thick, impenetrable whiteness cloaked the view. Even the tip of the wing was shrouded. This is where snow is made, thought Jannik. Up here, it's all the same.

Four and a half hours in, the plane landed at Kangerlussuaq. Jannik had mixed feelings about this. To his mind, Kangerlussuaq was nothing more than an airfield, a barren clearing in the earth; a scooped-up smudge of grey, surrounded by the ubiquitous snow, with a few dozen small buildings arranged in orderly straight lines. Everything there was in the service of the airport. Possibly the tiny settlement warranted further exploration, but Jannik couldn't think what he'd come across. All he'd ever seen of the place was the inside of the airport bar – where he'd waited, previously with his colleagues, while the planes were changed – plus an outdoor crossroads, a white-painted signpost, pointing in the direction of far-flung places such as Moscow, Tokyo, and New York.

On the other hand, this was one time he wouldn't have minded being stranded, despite the lack of distraction. But the weather here was better, more so than it had been in Copenhagen. A gentle wind cleared the air. Whatever snow there was had been swept to the perimeters. As the sun set the clouds broke and parted, and through a green wisp of the Aurora Borealis, Jannik could make out the stars in the sky. His onward journey was to run as scheduled.

Nuuk, at least, had a bit more going for it – there were shops, bars, a few museums – but like every settlement in Greenland, due to the hostile, impassable terrain, there was no land access between the sparsely distributed towns. Once the novelty of visiting Greenland's capital for the first time had worn off, even here Jannik was beginning to feel boxed in.

He stayed at the main hotel in town, the Hans Egede, remaining awake until well past midnight while he finished beta-checking for Synatech which, on a purely technical level, was finally to his satisfaction. But the program as a whole – a team effort from the IT department, also worked on by Birgita – was not how he would have written it. Delving into the coding, there seemed to be many parts which had no relevance. If the outsourcers needed this system to take on Kjær-Iversen's customer service function, it could hardly be worth their while. The maintenance required, the inevitable errors which even the inexperienced Jannik could foresee – neither of these would make it cost-effective. Surely Søndergaard could not have overlooked that?

Early the next morning, Jannik paid a visit to the data centre on the edge of town. Kristian, the site manager who greeted him, expressed some surprise that it was only Jannik who turned up.

"Don't tell me they've downsized and it's only you left," said Kristian, leading him through a narrow corridor to the control room.

"You're not a million miles off," replied Jannik. They reached the room and sat at a bank of monitors beneath a row of flickering fluorescent lights. "Ever heard

216

of Synatech?"

"Have I ever," said Kristian, turning on a machine. "They've spent the best part of five years working their way down the eastern seaboard. Gobbling up the competition. So, they're crossing the pond now?"

"It seems that way," said Jannik. "Although it's just outsourcing, for now. Customer Services. I'm just here to run through the spec."

Kristian considered for a moment. He was older than Jannik, a good decade more experienced, and was sure to have seen similar situations before. "You have code?" he asked.

"Sure," said Jannik. "I probably shouldn't be showing you this, but…" He took his laptop from his bag and jacked it into a monitor. After a few seconds, the lines flickered up on the screen.

Kristian whistled. "That's far too complicated for a customer service function," he said. He turned back to Jannik. "You beta-tested?"

"Yes," said Jannik. From above, a previously dormant fluorescent bulb popped to life, casting a fresh illumination on the computer screen.

Kristian scrolled down. "Look at these subroutines. They're whole systems in themselves. Here, here and…" he scrolled to almost near the bottom. "Here. They've designed it to do more. Much more."

Jannik squinted at the code. He had, of course, only beta-tested the customer service function, as had been required of him; task logs, productivity stats, status. But Kristian was right. How could he not have determined what all those hidden extras were? "So, what you're saying is…"

"There's outsourcing. And then there's *outsourcing*. If you catch my drift."

Jannik did.

"And I'm sorry to say…" Kristian looked up at Jannik; on his first solo assignment. "I think they've got you to do their dirty work."

Jannik nodded. He concluded his business with Kristian and left the server station with a sense of foreboding, dreading that afternoon's meeting with Synatech.

Back in the centre of Nuuk snow was falling again; a wet sleet which refused to settle. Temperatures were back to below zero. Jannik shivered in his sheepskin jacket as he made his way past the small shopping centre to the Hans Egede. The two reps from Synatech were due to be landing early that afternoon. Could the weather maybe keep them away?

It was no surprise to discover that *Immaqa Air* had yet again pulled through, no 'maybe' about it. So, the meeting in a few hours was still on. Jannik retired to his room, idly turned on the television, flicked through the channels, and turned it off again. He went to the window and stared outside for a while. The view wasn't particularly impressive; just a few buildings in the distance, pastel-blue rooftops, slate-grey office blocks. Snow continued to fall, but not as heavy as before. It was the sort which drifted in the air, swirling, never touching the ground. He turned away.

On his bed lay the laptop, snapped shut and switched off. Jannik looked at it, then walked over and turned it on. A short while later all those lines of code were displayed in front of him once more. This time, the symbols and commands no longer shuffled in kaleidoscopic patterns.

It occurred to him to try something. Those previously

218

mysterious blocks of code – several pages which had nothing to do with customer service – must, in some way, work by themselves. He tried running one separately. An error message immediately flashed up. He tried the other, then the next, then the final one. Each time: different error messages. He looked at them more closely, going through them line by line. No wonder he could previously foresee errors. They weren't actually finished.

It was now obvious what the meeting was for. If Synatech had the lock, Jannik was to deliver the key. And as soon as they had the data they needed, they'd have the entire infrastructure of Kjær-Iversen; systems, access codes, financial forecasts, the lot. It wouldn't just be the twelve people in Customer Service in danger of losing their jobs.

He found himself hovering his finger over 'delete'. His eyes did a three-way glance between the code, his finger and the button. So far, he felt all he ever did was to rectify other people's mistakes. Now Søndergaard, alongside all the other share-owners, was about to make the biggest mistake of all. All Jannik would have to do was press downwards...

...no, he thought. What good would that do? They'd know immediately. They're experts. Besides it'd be backed up elsewhere. And Søndergaard would find out soon enough. Then they'd find some other ignorant, willing patsy to obliviously operate under the radar.

He sighed, switched off the laptop, and made his way to conference room 59.

At five o'clock, two young men in jeans and T-shirts walked in. Jannik, having dressed smartly for the occasion, rose to meet them, doing his best to hide his surprise. They were barely older than he was. Younger, maybe.

"Brad," the first said.

"Josh," said the other.

Jannik introduced himself as they shook hands. "So, they just sent you two?" he asked.

"We're the couriers, I guess," said Josh. "Ones with Computer Science degrees, but, hey."

"So, Jannik," said Brad. "What do you have for us that's so important it couldn't be mailed?"

Each had a laptop, which they plugged in and fired up. Josh wired up a connector, just a single line leading from all three machines to a small metallic hub which Jannik couldn't identify. Within seconds, Josh turned to Brad.

"All done?" said one.

"All done," said the other.

"Already?" said Jannik. "Are you not going to run any checks?"

"Completed," said Brad. "Josh here," he said, turning to his companion, "is a whizz."

Josh patted the small, mysterious cube of titanium. "Runs the necessary in a tenth of the time at a twentieth of the expense. Although," he turned to Brad, "top secret, right buddy?"

"Right on."

Bigger, better, faster, thought Jannik. And for what?

"Anyway," said Brad as the two Americans unplugged and clicked shut their computers, "short but sweet. Hardly worth the expense, but hey, what do we know? Have a nice stay."

"Thanks," said Jannik. The two young men made their exits and Jannik was left alone. The whole thing had taken less than five minutes.

Perhaps those lads were right. What *did* they know? About as much as each other, Jannik reckoned. Which really, when it came down to it, wasn't much at all.

On previous visits to Nuuk, Jannik had spent evenings in the hotel bar, or in bars or restaurants downtown, with colleagues. Now he was on his own, there seemed little point in doing anything. The only person he knew in the city was Kristian, but he didn't have his number. That left Brad and Josh, who on the face of it were friendly enough, but they didn't appear to be staying at the Hans Egede, and Jannik hadn't asked them about their arrangements. At any rate, the temperature outside had dropped further, the wet sleet becoming a blizzard. So, it was to be a quiet night in before his flights back the next day.

But he couldn't relax. Something was nagging him. He called Birgita from the hotel phone.

"Oh, it's you," she said from down the line. "I wasn't expecting you to check in." She sounded tired. Jannik realised he had forgotten the four hour time difference, but then decided to continue playing dumb. It somehow seemed appropriate.

"We don't have to outsource Customer Services," said Jannik. "We can save money, just by rewriting our software and using it ourselves. People can keep their jobs. Surely that's better than letting people go?"

There were a few moments silence at the other end of the line. "I'm sorry, Jannik," said Birgita. "That really isn't how it works. All I should say is…"

"I should look around for something else?"

Birgita paused again. "Yes," she said at last. "That's what I would do."

221

"Enjoy your dividend," said Jannik. He hung up before he had a chance to regret it.

Immaqa Air had come up trumps again; Jannik's flight back to Copenhagen via Kangerlussuaq had departed on time, although for a while it looked touch and go, with the snow settling on the ground and icy winds driving down from the north. However, by the time the plane touched down at Kangerlussuaq, a bumpy landing which shook the craft from nose to tail, the winds had mutated into gales. A piercing snowdrift blew into the passengers' faces as they disembarked onto the tarmac.

It was to be a two hour wait until their connecting flight, but Jannik, as he made his way to the terminal, guessed it would be longer. He passed by the crossroads. Copenhagen, according to the signpost, was four hours and fifteen minutes away. It may as well have been a lifetime.

It was as good as confirmed when he made it inside. Passing the Air Greenland representative at the departures desk, the same girl who'd checked him in at Copenhagen, she looked up at him in recognition, and shrugged. She wore the resigned yet stoic expression with which regular travellers with the airline were so familiar.

"Today we are *Immaqa Air*?" he asked her.

"Maybe," said the girl.

"Maybe maybe?" said Jannik.

"*Immaqa.*"

Outside, the snowstorm was picking up. Blurred arrows of white darted horizontally through the frosty arctic evening.

"Can you answer something else for me?" Jannik said.

"Of course," said the girl.

"You speak Greenlandic. Is it true that you have over a hundred words for snow?"

The girl smiled, pleased to have something else to talk about. "No," she said. "It's a popular myth. We have one word for snow in the air, *qanik*, and another for snow on the ground, *aput*. That's all."

"Thank you," said Jannik. "I suspected as much."

"You're welcome," said the girl. She glanced out the window. "Good luck."

With the weather worsening, Jannik made his way through the small airport to the adjoining Hotel Kangerlussuaq.

He thought of Søndergaard, and how he would justify what was going to happen to the business and its employees. He'd probably declare it to be best for the company: the obvious course of action for the changeable climate.

On the runway outside Jannik spotted a small plough, scooping and sweeping as it rumbled its way from one end to the other. Something occurred to him. Surely there were three types of snow, rather than two? *Aput*, for snow on the ground; *qanik*, for snow in the air; and, the third, a wordless definition: snow that was swept aside.

Jannik found the hotel, checked in, headed upstairs to one of the few remaining rooms, and swiped his keycard.

The door stayed resolutely shut. He tried again. The light upon the lock maintained an obstinate red.

Come on, thought Jannik. Give me a break.

He tried again, and again.

When on the seventh attempt the lock still wouldn't release, hot blood rushed to Jannik's temples. Under his sheepskin jacket, he'd broken a sweat; a thin film of it dampened his collar, tickling his neck. Breathing in sharply through his teeth, he was surprised to find he'd balled his fist, ready to strike the door.

Never before had he wanted to hit anyone or anything. Baulking at this unfamiliar, aggressive pose, he shut his eyes, relaxed his hand, and leaned to, his forehead resting against the cool timber.

No longer would he let himself be subject to forces beyond his control.

He stepped back, breathed out, and slowly swiped his keycard one more time. With a gentle click, the light emitted green and the door creaked open.

Inside, the bedroom window looked out upon a dark, austere landscape. Lightning forked the sky. As the storm raged, Jannik sighed, pulled down the blinds, and turned away.

Immaqa, he said to himself as he lay upon the bed. *Immaqa.*

About the author

Mike Scott Thomson's stories have been featured by a number of publications, including *The Fiction Desk*, *Litro*, *Prole*, and Momaya Press. Competition successes include the runner up prizes in both InkTears (2012) and Writers' Village (2013). In 2014 he won the inaugural 'To Hull and Back' humorous short story competition. Based in Mitcham, Surrey, he works in broadcasting. You can find him online at www.mikescottthomson.com.

The Winter Cuckoo

Shirley Hammond

It was the Tiger's fault.

Our neighbour is proud of her nickname. She is aware of her elegantly striped hair and the feline slant to her eyes. She also employs, to effect, the purring vowels she developed for minor parts in television soaps twenty years ago – before she gave up her career for Barney's millions and an escape to the country.

What she doesn't know is that she has earned the name, as far as the village is concerned, in two other ways. The first by her somewhat predatory attitude towards men (wasted on Gwyn, however) and the second because she never – ever – calls round to see anybody without having designs on their resources.

It is a freezing cold Valentine's Day morning when she tells us the reason for her visit.

"It's about my friend Jason Knight. You might have heard of him. He's making quite a name for himself as a sculptor. So clever. And such good company."

"Never heard of him," says Gwyn, who, since retirement from town planning, spends most of his time growing vegetables and soft fruit in the garden.

"Well, sculpture isn't really your thing, I know that. But his reputation is starting to travel way beyond the artists' colony here. The only thing is, he's split up from his girlfriend and has had to move out of their house. So sad."

"He had no choice in the matter?" I ask. I used to work in social services.

"Oh no, nothing like that," the Tiger says quickly, "just grown apart over the years. But the arguments weren't helping his creativity. He needs his own space.

And I suddenly thought – how wonderful if you could let out your flat to him."

We have a small, self-contained flat on the second floor of our house, which we let out to holidaymakers in season. It's popular with families, being cheaper than a cottage, and within walking distance of the beach.

"Why can't you have him?" Gwyn asks.

"Oh darlings – you know I couldn't. What would people say, with Barney having died so recently?"

Barney was thirty years her senior. His earthly career collapsed last summer. The Tiger continues to occupy their enormous former rectory with every appearance of enjoyment and a Polish couple who do all the work.

She changes tack.

"I thought I was doing you a *favour*!" she mews. "He would be paying you. And he'll be out all day. He'll be no trouble."

"I suppose we could let him have it until Easter," I say, turning to Gwyn. "On a weekly let. I would have to charge for doing his laundry."

There isn't a washing machine or tumble dryer in the flat.

"Only if he limits himself to two suitcases," says Gwyn. "And we'll have to meet him first."

Jason Knight turns out to be a tall, quietly spoken man of about forty, with greying hair tied back in a ponytail, a long moustache, and several tattoos which look like signs of the Zodiac. He wears a lot of silver jewellery, and a vintage sweatshirt with a picture of Che Guevara; but, on the whole, seems relatively inoffensive, and accepts our terms.

On the day he arrives, it is clear that Gwyn's edict regarding luggage has been ignored.

Heavy-looking grey clouds gather, as a traveller acquaintance of his brings a truck to the front of the house and empties a mountain of possessions on to the drive. Being woolly liberals, we fail to say anything at this point. It takes Jason an hour to get everything up the stairs. No, he does not want any help.

He refuses a cup of tea.

We take up a plate of home-made Welsh cakes. He does not say thank you. Over his shoulder, before he gently but firmly shuts the door in our faces, we can see that the whole flat has apparently disappeared under overflowing containers.

For the rest of the day, and late into the night, our quiet domestic pursuits are enlivened by muffled sounds of thunder and unidentifiable crashes above us as he settles in.

In the morning, he leaves the house in a snowstorm, looking like an astronaut in a heavily padded suit. On his return, he strips off to his underpants in the porch. This has large windows on three sides, which means he is in full view of all the neighbours. He proceeds to hang up his now dripping outerwear and almost equally sodden undergarments on the curtain rails, having first taken off the curtains and piled these in a heap by the front door.

Pints of icy, muddy water drip on to the radiators, the carpet, and my cherished bowls of paperwhite narcissi. Outside, the light is failing. A solidarity of enemy snowflakes – now packed together in their frost-biting millions inches deep – surrounds us.

I go upstairs and remind him that I am happy to wash and dry his apparel. I will ensure that all items are returned to him in the state he would like to find them, and add the cost to the weekly charge. He glowers, and says nothing.

That same evening we can hear repetitive guitar chords accompanied by sounds of an animal in pain.

"He didn't smuggle in a dog, did he?" I ask.

"He'd better not have," says Gwyn. "We'll check tomorrow."

The central heating system serves the whole house. During the night we become aware from its familiar sounds that the hot water appears for some reason to be on continually.

We cannot sleep because of the noise above. Putting on our dressing gowns, we go quietly up the stairs. A white mist curls its tentacles under the door of the flat. We knock; but cannot make ourselves heard. Gently, we push open the unlocked door. We gaze into the living room.

The thick white mist damply embraces everything within reach. It is created by hot water running into the kitchen sink and meeting below-freezing air from the wide open window.

In the armchair, strumming his guitar, surrounded by pink fairy lights, Jason is wailing tuneless songs of loss to the cruel, black uniformed night sky – now studded with a million diamonds. Suspended, shadowy steel mobiles in gargoyle shapes weave around his head as the wind blows. He does not see us.

We withdraw. Gwyn goes downstairs and switches off the boiler. Half an hour later, we are able to settle down to sleep.

After Jason has left the house in the morning, we take the master key and go up to inspect.

We discover the following:

There are black masks stuck on to all the kitchen cupboards.

Numerous Christmas decorations have been hammered into the ceiling.

One wall is covered with sellotaped photographs of a naked Jason, from babyhood to the present day.

There are bowls of smelly, decaying bulbs everywhere.

A still is happily bubbling away by the sink.

In the main bedroom, an extremely graphic picture of a sheela-na gig is above the bed; next to a picture of the Tiger in her glory days. A half empty bottle of red wine stands on the bedside table. The rest of the wine appears to have been used to create abstract patterns on the white bed linen.

We go into the second bedroom. There we find the piece de resistance.

The adult sized bunk beds are serving as cold frames for feathery green plants commonly associated with police scrutiny.

"I shall kill the Tiger," says Gwyn.

"What will the agency say?" I wonder.

"Nothing good," says Gwyn. "What a nightmare."

"Knightmare with a K," I say. "Take some pictures."

Gwyn discovers from a phone call to a friend in the probation service that the initiated can transform the rotting bulbs into hallucinogens by means of the still. He moves them out – and the feathery green plants – on to the snowy drive outside the house. He stuffs most of the Knightmare's possessions back into plastic bags, and dumps them outside too. The wind chill factor increases.

The Knightmare is not pleased on his return. "Those plants will die!" he shrieks. "You're damaging my property."

"And you've been damaging ours" says Gwyn. "Get the hell out. Now. And I'll have your keys back too."

The Knightmare discovers to his chagrin that a weekly let, especially when you are in receipt of personal services (laundry, not sex) does not constitute a tenancy agreement.

He also discovers, later on, that arranging for spare copies of house keys to be cut achieves nothing as long as the owners of the property have had the foresight to get the locks changed immediately after eviction.

We remove the glue, re-varnish the cupboards, replace the bed linen and repaint the walls.

We dine out on the photographs for months.

The Tiger complains of boredom and isolation. She sells the rectory and moves back to London. Apparently, she has a new friend – a successful screenwriter – who can offer her an alternative to slumming it in the sticks. Gwyn says we should sell him our story.

"We could afford a new greenhouse with proper heating then," I tell him.

"Yes" he muses. "I could do a lot with one of those."

About the author
Shirley Hammond is one of a dozen committed members of a creative writing group in Tenby, Pembrokeshire, run by author Judith Barrow. Several of her short stories, plays and poems have reached competition shortlists. Her experiences of country living in retirement – after a varied public sector career spanning education, social housing and social services, and looking after holidaymakers from all walks of life over recent years – have provided her with much interesting material. However, she holds to the adage that if a story is worth telling, it is worth embroidering...

Index of Authors

Other Publications by Bridge House

Something Hidden

edited by Debz Hobbs-Wyatt and Gill James

There is something hidden, something darker and something
challenging behind that placid veneer of calmness we so often
see in everyday life. We asked for something a little darker for
our latest short story competition. The entrants certainly
supplied that. In this anthology we've collected the strongest.
Each of the stories makes you think.

"Loved this story (*Home*) in particular as it resonated with me
but all of the stories were enjoyable and well weitten."
(*Amazon*)

Order from www.bridgehousepublishing.co.uk

Paperback: ISBN 978-1-907335-31-0
eBook: ISBN 978-1-907335-33-4

Light in the Dark

edited by Gill James

We asked for stories that would make readers think. We
certainly got them. Some edge towards the dark, though all
have some closure and turn back towards the light. Just as
Advent time rushes towards the darkest days so that we can
return to the light, these twenty-four stories bring light into
our dark.

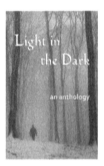

Order from www.bridgehousepublishing.co.uk

Paperback: ISBN 978-1-907335-37-2
eBook: ISBN 978-1-907335-38-9

Lightning Source UK Ltd.
Milton Keynes UK
UKOW06f1306201115

263172UK00001B/11/P